MURDER ON PINE MOUNTAIN

A WARM SPRINGS MYSTERY
BOOK TWO

D. SMITH

Murder on Pine Mountain by D. Smith

Book 2 in the Warm Springs Mystery series

Published by Kingfisher Press

Fairview, North Carolina, United States of America

Visit the author's website at www.douglaspsmith.com

Copyright © 2025 Douglas P. Smith

Cover design by Getcovers

Print ISBN: 978-1-964344-04-1

"Good morning hero." Lottie only called me that because she knew it irked me. But it was now part of our banter, so I didn't mind as much.

"Hey Lottie."

"You wanting the usual?"

"No, this morning I'll take avocado toast with a side of roasted chia seeds and brie. And an algae smoothie with pickled quail eggs."

"Whatever that is, hero, you ain't getting it here. What you are getting is the usual."

"Thanks, Lottie, that'll be just fine."

"You know it." She left to put the order in. I guess I should be honored that she considered me a regular. She wasn't as nice to new people. Mable's Diner was my go-to place a couple of times a week for breakfast or brunch in Warm Springs. I attended more often than in the past, since my new business was next door.

She brought me a large biscuit filled with scrambled eggs, cheese, and bacon, all melted together inside. I ate my customary half. The rest would be for lunch, mine plus some shared with my cat. Kat would demand a taste but would not eat much. I was also watching her cholesterol.

"You making any money next door?" Lottie asked when she came by to refill my coffee.

"That would be a definite no."

"Not much of a mystery, hero. We don't exactly have an erudite populace hereabouts."

"Why Lottie, I didn't know you were a wordsmith."

"What you don't know would fill a search engine."

"Probably. But I'm still young enough to think I know everything."

She snorted and moved on. I went back to brooding on my latest endeavor. I had been getting bored in Warm Springs. A few months ago, a small retail space opened up in the same sprawling brick building that Mable's was in. I took over the lease and began what might be the worst idea I'd had in a while. Or the best, given enough time. It was a bookstore. Even if it wasn't profitable, it gave me and Kat a place to go during the day.

Unfortunately, I didn't have many customers. Most came through to see Kat. Or were customers coming out of Mable's Diner and needed some extra time to digest. I also got to see the huge dirty underbelly of the book world. I knew about that world from the other side, from writing non-fiction textbooks and historical fiction novels. But the initial business of running a bookstore was maddening. At least for me, at this early stage. Trying to decide what books to stock, whether ones I liked or bestsellers, to keeping up with inventory, and dealing with various wholesalers and publishers kept me busy in a bad way. I just wanted to sit in my bookstore with Kat and watch books fly off the shelves. I knew every new business startup was like this, feeling overwhelmed with new processes and being unprofitable. I was getting too old for this, though.

It sounded so cool, owning a bookstore. Like owning a famous restaurant, or an established bed and breakfast. I should have known better. Every town should have a great bookstore, but someone besides me should own it. Same as swimming pools, horses, and airplanes. All things your best friend or neighbor owns, but you get to play with without ownership responsibility. But it was something Emma and I had talked about semi-seriously for years. I knew I did not want the bed and breakfast or restaurant, but maybe we could have done a bookstore together. Except now I was doing it alone.

I was trying to make the store successful. Even before opening, I had spent time thinking of different ways to bring in customers. I did it even more since opening, when the tedious details of the business allowed me time. Last week I scheduled a local author event. Donna Childers lived in the area and wrote romantic mystery under a pen name. She had come by and introduced herself. While she wandered around the store, I checked and saw she was doing well enough online. Kat also followed her around, which was an important endorsement. I invited Donna to have a reading and book signing at the store. She agreed, and I did some advertising. Donna could meet some local fans and maybe I could move some books. It wasn't the worst way of marketing. Nor the worst way of getting to see Donna again.

Two days ago, on Saturday, Donna had arrived at the store. We were both full of hope. I helped her bring in a table and we set it up. She had a covering, a banner, her books, some freebies to give out, and a luscious silver platter of pastries. I did my best to be polite and not notice how attractive she was. She had long chestnut hair, bright blue eyes, and a mischievous smile. Which had nothing to do with her being the first author to present at the store.

Unfortunately, one of us, probably me, had forgotten to lock the table legs. An enthusiastic patron bumped the table... and just like that I had the first official book signing disaster at my store. Donna was great about everything and so were the customers. The remaining pastries hit the floor and some of the books got scuffed, but no major harm was done. I was appalled, but Donna kept on going without a skip. That was an admirable quality.

Donna commenced her reading as two dozen customers settled in their seats. Her writing was funny, and she had excellent timing and rhythm telling her stories. All the fans were entranced. Then the power went off.

I had some candles in the desk drawer, so she finished in candlelight, which wasn't the worst way to end a signing. I felt bad about the whole thing and offered to buy her dinner. She accepted, and we had plans to go to Woodbury on Friday night. Kat, the matron of the store, also liked her, so that was a positive. Although it could have been all the pastry crumbs Kat got to eat off the floor after the table disaster. The little dustmop had developed a bit of a sweet tooth.

"Hey Romeo, where you taking Donna to eat?" Lottie roused me from my remembrance.

"If you already know about the dinner, you should know the where."

"I heard Woodbury, but I know you know better than that."

"Uh, what?"

"That place ain't great. Donna's a class act. Do better, Romeo."

"OK, what would you suggest?"

"I heard you can cook. Why don't you cook for her?"

"That might be presumptuous."

"Nah, it's not a date. You just owe her for the fiasco you put her through."

"Lottie, you might just be the most vexatious person in this town."

"Why thank you, Romeo. That makes my day." If nothing else, I at least had a new nickname. I wasn't sure it was better than hero, though.

I paid the tab, put the half of a stuffed biscuit in a paper bag, and got a smirk from Lottie. Then I left for the long trip back to work. Perhaps fifty steps. I unlocked the door and turned the sign on the door around to indicate the store was open. Now I had to worry about where to take Donna on Friday or ask her over to my house. I was not good at this, and Lottie had realized it. Attacking the weakest animal in the herd, me. Well, time to be decisive and deal with it.

I called Donna and she answered. She was writing, but ready to take a break. We made small talk for two minutes.

"Say Donna, instead of going to Woodbury on Friday, I'd like to offer the choice of coming to my house for dinner."

"James, I'd love to come over. The only cooked meals I get are my own and I'm about tired of my cooking."

"Great, and I know how you feel. Is there anything in particular you don't like? I'll make sure and leave it off the menu."

"No, nothing comes to mind. I'm sure whatever you come up with will be fine." Wonderful, that gave me nothing to go on. Chicken, seafood, steak? Pasta or salad? Vegetarian? I was going to have to wing it, pun intended. But I'd never serve wings on a date. Or a friendly get together.

"That sounds good. What time would you like to come over?"

"I'll be there around six."

"I'm on the Roosevelt campus, if you remember."

"Yes, the house beside the police station. I know where it is."

"Great, see you then."

"I'm looking forward to it. Bye."

That went better than expected. Maybe Lottie was right. Now I was sitting in awe that I was surrounded by books at my bookstore. It made all the hassle worth it for a few moments. Followed by panic that I hadn't gotten the right orders in, or that the local and state taxes were incorrect. Then Kat sat by me and demanded some neck rubs. A customer came in and bought a book. I was fine again for a while. It must be shop owner's regret or something.

I still had plenty of alone time to ruminate over my impending dinner. Should I serve wine or just tea? Wine might be seen as too forward, but not serving it would look cheap. I might be overthinking everything. For food, seafood was out. I could do good things with salmon or scallops, but not everyone liked seafood. Steak perhaps, but the past decade I had put away most red meat. I didn't trust the quality anymore for various reasons. Finally, I decided to go simple and elegant. A green salad with homemade ranch dressing extra light on the garlic and onion; roast chicken with green beans and broiled new potatoes. I could kick it up a notch with fresh herbs and spices. I once had the same dish in Paris and wanted mine to equal the flavor. For that, I needed a good light red wine, plus I would brew some ice tea in case she didn't want wine.

Kat came down from a shelf once she smelled the biscuit. She would have to wait a while. After a quick belly rub, she went to the window to sit in the sun and draw customers. She was better at marketing than me.

CHAPTER TWO

Wandering down the campus lane on a sunny morning, I entered the cafeteria. "Hey George," I said to the large man who ran the place.

"Hi James. We still on for tomorrow?"

"Sure are, since the garden won't weed itself. You enjoying the greens?"

"We are. Enough are coming in that we can use them in our cooked menu. A shame we can't put them on the salad bar."

"I know, the state regulations are convoluted. Guess they don't trust us to grow and serve raw foods."

"Maybe Ison can get us some relief."

"I'll ask him. He's sitting over there." I picked up a

couple of breakfast items and headed over to Ison's table. He was an administrator on campus and had pushed me into volunteering to start a campus garden.

"Good morning Ison."

"Morning James. You still complaining about the state regulations?"

"You know it. I understand the intent, but I have more food safety experience than anyone in the current state government. I know what can and cannot be served."

"Doesn't matter, as you know. But maybe we can get it relaxed. You willing to train the garden people?"

"Whatever it takes. The salad bar would get an upgrade with all the stuff we could put on it."

"Go ahead and get me a plan. I'll see if I can get it approved."

"Thanks. Say, I have not seen Benjamin sulking around recently and giving me looks like he wanted to wipe me off the bottom of his shoe."

"He's been reassigned. Still around, unfortunately, even after those embarrassing documents showed up."

"Reassigned? He should have been fired. That tells me something."

"Yes, that his schemes were not solely his own. He might even be up for a promotion this year."

"Somebody in state government in Atlanta was in on it. I hate politics and sycophants."

"Most assuredly. But at least the plans to develop campus with condominiums have been put on hold if not discarded."

"Getting it slowed down was about all I could hope for.

In two or three years the economy can change, and financial backers pull out."

"Or an even worse developer can take it over and push it through."

"Thanks, Ison, for that ray of sunshine."

"My pleasure. It seems the big development up on Pine Mountain is also on hiatus."

"Same type of deal as the campus condos. Hopefully it will slow down enough that inertia will kill it."

"Interesting how both things happened at once. Almost as if they were connected."

"Ison, you know I did it. There, I have confirmed your suspicions."

"I never doubted it was anyone but you. The only question I ever had is where you got the documents."

"From the source. He didn't mind at the time."

"Ah, the gentleman who so graciously killed himself in your house after drinking your poisoned whiskey."

"In my defense, he was about to shoot me in the head and stage my suicide. I guess it didn't work out the way either of us planned."

"I would say it did work out for the best, however. Just rewards for him killing his partner and dumping her body here in our lake."

"I agree. She didn't deserve that, but he certainly deserved a bad end for what he did."

"I'll bluntly change the subject. How's the bookstore doing?"

"About what you would expect a new independent bookstore to do in a small town."

"That bad, huh?"

"But it is worth it to provide the community with a bastion of literacy and culture."

"Amazing. You said that with a straight face."

"I've been practicing. I can use it as a sales pitch for the next sucker that wants to buy my bookstore."

"Good luck with that."

I kept that exchange in my head as I pedaled into town. I was on the bike since Kat was going to work with me and her carrier was strapped to the back rack. Although not lucrative, I really did like having a bookstore in town. I would keep it open as long as I could. After all, I didn't need the money as far as steady income and it gave me something to do.

Inside the store, I let Kat out and she proceeded to re-sniff and rub on everything within reach. After she got bored, she jumped on top of a shelf where she could see the window and door and began licking herself. Business as usual.

I had brought us lunch, so we didn't have to go out. After that I sat outside on a bench I had placed under the window while Kat took another nap. Buyers were slow to come in this morning. Maybe the afternoon would pick up. The door to Mable's opened and Lottie came out with a small plate loaded with a slice of pie. I didn't care which flavor since they were all good. Today it looked like coconut. Lately we had been meeting like this. She gave me pie and I provided the straight man for her acid wit. We both got what we wanted.

"You get that dinner date fixed?"

"I did, thanks to your wisdom. She is coming over to the house and I'll cook dinner."

"In that case, here's your pie."

"You weren't going to give it to me otherwise?"

"No reward for stupidity. Can't provide nourishment for the demented to keep surviving. You get the basic training like Pavlov's dog. Otherwise you might rub off on others and then where would we be?"

"A bunch of pie-fed idiots?"

"Exactly. Town is too small for that."

"It is apparently also too small for a bookstore."

"You aren't going to go belly up on my lease are you?"

"Your lease? I have a lease with Dogwood Enterprises."

"Yeah, that is one of my companies."

"What? I thought the Atlanta couple that owns Mable's was the lease owner."

"Nope, this is my building. Bought it cheap a long time ago. Also have that one across the street with the clothing shop on one side and the antique store on the other side."

"Lottie, I had no idea. Why are you working at Mable's?"

"Need something to do or I'll go crazy. Decided to help out the Atlanta couple. I think of it as lease assurance."

"Well then, I don't feel nearly as bad mooching this pie from you."

"Oh, you are paying for the pie. I've been running a tab. Can't have Mable's go belly up from your pie obsession."

"Ouch. The richest lady in town is pushing pie on me like a drug, then secretly charging me."

"If you don't like capitalism you can move back to Europe. And don't be calling me a lady."

"That is what you took from that?"

"Uh oh, here he comes."

The conversation paused while we watched Millard zip into town in his chariot. He passed us, then spun around in the fancy, barely street legal utility vehicle, and parked in front of us with a big smile.

"I cannot believe you gave him that thing. He's eighty going on eight."

"He gets a kick out of it, though. Good to see him out and about."

"He's terrorizing the town. Won't leave us good folks alone."

"Is he here for the food or the server?"

"Keep a civil tongue in your head. Otherwise, I'll raise your pie price."

"I don't know what you're charging me now, so I won't notice the increase."

Millard was unbuckled and carefully stepped up onto the sidewalk. His waistcoat, or vest, of the day was green silk with blue and white windmills. Very Dutch. "Look here, my two favorite people sitting here with pie," he said.

"It's a nice day, isn't it, Millard?" I asked innocently.

"That it is."

"I've got to go check on Kat. She'll be looking for her snack. Here, Millard, take my spot."

"I believe I will. Thank you James. Hello, Lottie, how are you doing?" Millard carefully maneuvered up the steps. He had a bad hip.

"Just fine, Millard. Seems like you've gone another day and not killed yourself in that thing."

"Oh, it is safe enough. Top speed of this thing is the town limit, so I'll always be legal."

I went into the bookstore before I heard Lottie's reply.

Those two had known each other forever. Millard was always nice to her and she always gave him a hard time. But not as hard as she gave me. Maybe she was mellowing around him. He probably got better pie prices than I did.

I checked on some books on order, surfed the internet, and did some writing. The day was just slow. Even Mable's had a lighter than usual crowd for lunch. At four, I finally gave up and closed the store. I wheeled my bike from the back and put Kat in her carrier. I didn't know if she enjoyed the short mile on the bike, but so far she had not complained. Minutes later, we were at the house and Kat was lounging in the front yard.

I took off on my walk around campus, heading for the outer loop with all the abandoned cottages rotting into the encroaching forest. The Roosevelt Warm Springs campus was once a thriving community dedicated to helping polio patients, and later anyone with head, spinal cord or stroke injuries. Franklin D. Roosevelt started it and it was still active for treating patients. But the community built around the effort had deteriorated. Inexplicably, the state had disallowed anyone to lease or buy the many cottages once their original occupants left or died. Abandoned, they were in disrepair and crumbling into the dirt. An unexplained sin that nobody would answer for.

The overgrown yards still sported some colorful plantings grown wild. Large camellias in the winter and early spring, and various decorative shrubs planted more than fifty years ago. These were the cottages that Benjamin and his ilk had targeted for razing for a new condominium development. But that was scheduled for after the cottages were to be "renovated" in an illegal scheme to enrich a few people. One of the schemes that the murdering real estate agent was brokering before dying in my living room. Ironically, he also wanted my cottage. I had one of only a few on the campus with private ownership.

I kept walking and soon neared Millard's cottage. Another rare private residence he owned outright. The utility vehicle or UTV, basically an overgrown go-cart for adults I had given him so he could get around, was not at the house. He must still be in town talking to Lottie or grocery shopping. He also had a few old buddies he could now visit, so he might be playing cards with them. I would catch him on a walk later this week or see him in town. The UTV was a way for him to get out more without undue stress on his bad hip.

He was a former administrator on campus and mayor, so he knew lots of people and official secrets. I hung out on his front porch once or twice a week and cut the grass in his small front yard. He had also helped me with the investigation into Tammy Wilkins' murder last spring. The end of that investigation happened when the murder, her partner Joe Burgess, came to kill me and drank poisoned whiskey instead. Millard saw a truck by the lake at the time of her murder that ended up matching one driven by Joe.

Lottie, Mable's server and real estate mogul, had also helped a lot in the case. The former County Clerk, she knew everything and everyone, both personally and legally. I was beginning to think she had taken me on as an apprentice. Or maybe she needed somebody new to harangue. It worked for me because she took as good as she gave.

I continued my walk downhill and passed near the lake

where it had all started. That was where I first spotted Tammy's body. Today it was nice weather with the sun reflecting off the steel blue surface, broken only by a few floating geese and ducks. A handful of turtles found shallow spots to sun themselves. A calm and peaceful place, like most of campus. Overall, I was lucky to be living here.

CHAPTER THREE

I had bought my hundred-year-old house that had a guest cottage out back because of the location. The Roosevelt Warm Springs campus that I called RWS had most of what I was looking for in my early retirement situation. The house was also in good shape although it could use updates in the kitchen and bathrooms. A small guest cottage behind the house, however, was in poor shape and once I began internal demolition, it got worse. Termites had come and gone. The little annoyances had digested most of the usable wood inside the structure. I was left with beams, floor joists, and foundation bands of balsa wood. It was taking longer than expected and eating up the budget. I was still working on the walls and ceiling, but more slowly.

Meanwhile, I redirected some effort and money toward the master bath in the house. The standalone clawfoot tub had to go. It was not original and only a few years old. I needed a shower and had never been a tub person. The only issue was a large window in the middle of the long wall where the shower needed to be built. I considered removing it, but hated not having a window in the large bathroom. Another option was to replace the window with a small window high up on the wall for privacy. That would detract from the exterior of the house as the window was matched with two others on that wall. Plus, I would need to match the old siding to blend in the large hole with the existing siding.

My solution was to build a tile shower to include the existing window. The wood trim was replaced with tile, and a shower door of frosted glass was installed over the window opening. That protected the old wood window, let in light while retaining privacy, and I could open the door to reach the window, opening it when I wanted fresh air or to clean it. I wasn't sure if it would work long term, but so far it had.

It was garden day, so I pedaled over to the golf course. It was semi-famous and had hosted lots of celebrities, mostly from the 1930s and 1940s. Unfortunately, it suffered the same fate as many of the cottages. Abandoned fifteen years ago, it was only cut occasionally, and kept the vast deer population in grass. We had located the community or campus garden near the edge of the old course. We probably could have put it in the middle of a fairway, but I still had hopes the course would come back someday.

The volunteer garden had begun last spring. A date too late for the early greens, but we had good luck over the summer and fall with tomatoes, squash, beans, and peas. The okra and cucumbers did OK, but nothing special. This year we had put in early greens and had gotten lots of lettuce varieties, cabbage, kale, arugula and collards. We were an eclectic bunch. We were planting much of the same summer crops as last year. But first, we needed to weed some new ground that Wes had recently plowed. We had a three-year rotation plan for the site and were about to expand to plant a good stand of corn. We needed the fence to extend around the new area. Otherwise, the deer would decimate whatever we planted.

Our little group was Wes and Ernie from the grounds crew, Edna from the police department, George from the cafeteria, and me. Our newest member was Alisha from the hospital. She had joined us last year for a time, but then needed to take the fall off when she hit her eighth month of pregnancy.

She was here today with her baby in a carriage. When the little girl woke up, we had a mobile play pen she could stay in for a little while. We even had a pop-up canopy to keep her in the shade. Everyone took turns looking after her and Alisha. Alice was her name. Alisha said she was named after her grandmother. Alice was our official garden mascot.

Sometimes I saw Robert come and pick up Alisha and the baby after we finished. He never got out and talked to me or anyone else. I did not know if it was something to do fathering Alisha's baby when he was still married to Tammy, or if it was because I had caught Tammy's killer. Or maybe it was something else. Losing a wife was hard, as I knew. Alisha never said anything, and I did not ask. I was glad to have her and her baby girl and would never make her feel uncomfortable.

Today was tedious work. Everyone got a hoe and began chopping the weeds and grass popping up from the plowed ground. Then Edna began singing as the others joined in. Except for me, because my voice was pure fingernails on the chalkboard bad. Halfway down the plot, Alisha and Ernie grabbed rakes and pulled off the chopped greenery and smoothed the dirt. It would make the next round of planting easier next week.

Soon enough, we finished, and I walked back to my house. I fed myself and Kat and took a shower. Then it was in the chair for reading and contemplation. For Kat, it was all about the belly rub as she eagerly jumped up beside me.

Once again, I opened the legal-sized brown envelope with the Athens' return address. The pages I had sent in for analysis were included and sealed in a plastic wrap with air removed. There were several legal-sized white pages. Each had a copy of the barely legible letter horizontally placed on it. The translation was beside it. I had to turn the legal paper sideways to read it. Altogether, about seventy to eighty percent of the letter had been translated from its faded condition. Mostly from Albert's UGA lab, and a few small portions from my work. But there were several blocks of text that were illegible even with the hyperspectral analysis. A note inside the envelope explained the process the UGA lab had used, along with some explanations of why part of the text wasn't deciphered. It also included suggestions on who to send it to and the type of tests to run, if I needed it closer to one hundred percent complete. I read it again, for probably the tenth time since I had received it.

The original faded letter I had found under the guest cottage after cutting out the floor due to termite damage. While digging around in the dirt to remove debris and check the footings, my shovel had chinked against something glass. It was a slightly unusual glass jar with papers inside. The parts I could read were interesting enough that I took it to Athens to get the remainder clarified. Their work was enough to get me most of the pertinent information.

It was the account written in 1945 of a night on the Warm Springs campus. The year was illegible, but I thought it might be 1940. The author described a double murder. The two different murders were hidden by staging one as an accident, while the other murder victim went missing and was never found. My best rendition of the text was that a wealthy girl was on campus to receive therapy after contracting polio. It was what the campus was dedicated to do, so no surprise there. Her wealthy fiancé from up north arrived one day unannounced. He suspected she was romantically involved with someone local, a boy employed as a pusher for the wheelchair-bound. From the letter and its missing parts, I could not tell if she was involved with the boy or not. It did not matter to the fiancé and in his rage, he beat the local boy to death.

One part of the missing text was located in the middle of that description. But it seemed the fiancé then went to see the girl. Later that evening, she killed him with a knife. Again, I could not decipher whether she did it out of revenge, self-defense, or was meting out justice. If she was in a wheelchair, she must have been good with a knife or killed him in his sleep.

After the murder, the girl went to the letter's author for help. A plan was quickly put in place. A car picked up the fiancé's body from one of the cottages where he was killed. The body was hidden and buried but the exact location was not legible in the untranslated text. Next, the murdered local boy was put on the railroad tracks on the edge of town. As planned, it was hit by a train two hours later in the early morning. A terrible deed, but I realized it was necessary to cover up the first murder, in order to hide the second murder.

The campus and town mourned the tragic accident as the dead boy was popular in town and on campus. Meanwhile, the fiancé had a train ticket back home the next day, but obviously did not make the train. His parents contacted the girl a few days later inquiring about their son, who had not arrived back home. The girl assured the parents that their son had gotten on the train. A month later a search was conducted, and private detectives hired, but the fiancé was never found. He was presumed to have run off or been killed somewhere along the journey and thrown from the train.

The last part of the letter was the most mysterious part. Probably also the least likely part to be able to prove. It was an account of later events, and spoke to another murder and possible connections to World War II spy figures. I thought it unlikely, but then again, FDR was often on campus until his death in 1945.

Was any of this true, or was it someone's made-up story? Maybe it was the outline of a fictional manuscript or a summary of a book plot. But why hide it in a bottle under the guest cottage? There were other details in the letter that made it sound legitimate. But only some digging into old archives would lead to confirmation. I knew this kind of mystery would take hold of me until I solved it.

Although not my top priority, I had begun a list of where to start and what resources I might need. The local newspaper might have records that old. I had the fiancé's name and address, so I could look him up on the local paper in Connecticut as well. The girl's name should be on campus documents somewhere. I also knew there was an archive near Atlanta that had various old documents about the campus. Another archive with Warm Springs records was in New York. It was all going to be a manual endeavor, as I didn't think most of the records were digitized and searchable. I had not begun yet because opening and running the bookstore had consumed much of my free time. But maybe it was time to start. Millard was taking some shifts at the bookstore and I could at least get to the archive in Atlanta, called the Georgia Archives. Life was slowing down just enough to think it was doable.

CHAPTER FOUR

I found Bryan knocking on my front door bright and early. "Good morning, Chief," I greeted him after opening the door. Having the campus police chief visit me this early made me think something was wrong. But we were friends, and I knew he would not come over without a good cause. No reason to jump to a bad conclusion until I knew what was happening.

"Good morning, James."

"You want some strong coffee?"

"As much as I'd like to, no. I have a favor to ask you though, if you are not busy."

"Bryan, my current status rarely leads to anything busy. What do you need?"

"I have a situation on Pine Mountain, not far up up the ridge I could use help with. Unofficially, of course."

"Absolutely. I'll put my shoes on and we can go." But I already sensed this was something bad. I got my shoes and threw Kat a snack. She ate it and licked her paw as a sign of dismissal. I got into Bryan's official SUV and off we went. Leaving campus he turned right, then in Warm Springs he turned right again and began ascending the north side of Pine Mountain.

We passed the Little White House entrance. Just beyond was one of the big yellow signs announcing "Deer Crossing." No kidding, 10,000 acres of no hunting created an army of the critters. Who often strayed onto the road at night.

A few hundred yards further, he pulled over to the right side of the road. Three other cars were parked there. Two obvious police cars and one that looked unmarked.

"Bryan, can you tell me what this is about?"

"I'd rather not say anything yet. You will see for yourself in about three minutes. Once you take a look, I would appreciate your input. I would like you to be an unofficial consultant. As you might have guessed, this is a crime scene."

Ah, this was because I had told Bryan how I'd surveyed and evaluated the scene of a body I'd found on campus last year. I figured out quickly it had been a murder, although almost no one wanted to believe it.

"I can do that. But watch me so I don't mess up anything going in."

"It is just a short walk over to the edge of the woods. I'll tell you when to stop so you won't affect the scene."

I followed him over to the woods. The grass along the roadside was what I called "chigger height." Perfect for the little red mites from hell to crawl up a pants leg and inflict five days of ceaseless itch on the nether regions. I made a mental note to take a shower when I got home.

The edge of the woods which caught the most sun grew thick scrub pines. They hid whatever was behind in the more open hardwoods. Just into the woods was a blue tarp covering a mound. One that was suspiciously the same size as a human.

"I know you are getting here a little late, as some officers have already walked around. But do you notice anything either obvious or unusual, from the road over to the tarp?" Bryan asked.

"This roadside so far looks like what could be any of a few thousand miles of middle Georgia roads. Weeds along the road, then these small pines, with shorter weeds, pine straw, and trash under the canopy where we are standing. Lot of road noise but can't really see anything because the pine limbs are growing down close to the road to get the sun. Looks like a tarp covering something about the size of a human body about twenty feet over there."

"Anything else?"

"That covers most of my preliminary observation. I'll have more to add shortly. I suppose this is about to get real messy."

"What do you mean?"

"If that is a body over there, then I'm estimating it is laying on about three different jurisdictions."

"Yeah, that could be a problem. That is why I wanted to

get you out here early on. In about an hour, this will be party central."

"As I understand it you have campus and some of the surrounding state park." Bryan nodded as I continued. "The Little White House is through those trees and is a different state jurisdiction. And the Warm Springs city limit ends about here. Which then becomes county jurisdiction. I revise my earlier statement as there could be four jurisdictions represented with the new Warm Springs police department."

"All that is true. Without a survey we won't know who gets the case. I'm expecting a lot of bluster and nonsense in the next hour. I'm here obviously, and the older officer in the blue uniform is the new chief and so far the only officer for Warm Springs. He is John Dixon, a decent guy and retired Atlanta policeman. Until he gets a department, I'm still in charge of the town, though. I expect the county sheriff is on the way. Jefferson Jackson, who we call J.J., although there are also a lot of other unsavory names to describe him."

"Can I see the body?"

"Yes, but don't get too close. Five feet away should do."

Bryan moved closer to the body and took off the tarp. A middle-aged, average size man lay on the ground. Very dead. I squatted down and looked back at the road. "I don't see any drag marks."

"None were noted."

"Either one really big man or two guys carried him in and dropped him. See any footprints?"

"No, but the ground isn't right. We thought we had one back by the road but not sure yet."

"The body must not have been here too long."

"Why do you say that?"

"Only a few fire ants so far. A couple more hours and it will be covered. They are hungry this time of year. But the coroner should be able to tell you a lot more." I saw a wound and blood on the upper leg, but no other signs of what killed him.

"Is it possible to turn him over?"

"Should be. We've already photographed the body on this side. Hey Steve, can you help me turn him over?"

A deputy came over wearing gloves and handed a pair to Bryan. He put them on and the two of them turned the body. Rigor mortis was setting in because the limbs were stiffening. I didn't know much about human rigor, but I had studied it in other animals. Time to add humans to my reading list. But I knew human red muscle took longer than white muscle to progress into rigor, then hit full rigor by twenty-four hours. The body was probably a few hours dead.

I saw two holes in the chest, one in the right thigh. The thigh wound had gone through, so that is what I saw on the back of the leg. But something was off.

"Bryan, it looks like he was shot twice in the chest and once in the leg. But the wounds are not the same age."

"What do you mean?"

"He's wearing a light shirt, and you can see the two small holes and the blood soaking the shirt. The leg wound, though, it looks like powder burns on the jeans. Maybe because of that or the jeans, the blood looks darker, which would make it older. It might also be the difference in the arterial blood color of the chest wounds versus venous blood on the leg, but I doubt it. The leg wound was a skill shot made to cause a lot of pain without hitting the bone or artery. Also means he was killed elsewhere and dumped here."

"I have a lot of questions about what you just said. The main one being how you know what powder burns look like. But that can wait until we get back to the office."

"Then you are really not going to like what I say next. You need to check the fingers, toes, and teeth for trauma."

"What am I looking for?"

"You'll know it when you see it."

"OK, deputy, let's look at the fingers. I'll take the right hand." There was nothing unusual.

"I'll look at the teeth," Bryan said. A few seconds later, he finished. "I don't see anything I'd consider trauma. Teeth are in good shape."

Bryan stepped back. "Let's get some more pictures before taking off his shoes." Another deputy came over with a camera and spent nearly five minutes taking pictures from every angle.

"Alright, I'm taking off his shoes," Bryan said. I was expecting the worst since the shoes were untied. Bryan pulled off the right shoe first, then the sock. Everything looked normal. Then he took off the left shoe and had to pull more than the other shoe. It came free, and the sock was full of blood. It looked like a bag of squashed strawberries. One of the deputies stepped away and emptied his breakfast in the bushes. Bryan's face was white when he stepped back to where I waited. I noticed he had not removed the sock.

"James, that is disgusting. You're right, now I have more serious questions. You've seen this before."

"We should have this conversation elsewhere."

"I agree, and I'll have to insist on getting answers."

"I'll be around most anytime. I need to step back and walk over there and then uphill for a minute. Will that be OK and not affect the scene?"

"Go ahead. We'll get your shoe print, so we can exclude it if we find any suspect prints."

I went back toward the road to check on something I had seen in the scrub. Then I moved uphill along the tree line along the right of way. I saw another marker. Looking at a satellite map on my phone, I did the correlation and figured out the body was in the city limits of Warm Springs and in the park limits. It was so close to the line that maybe the head was outside the city limits and in the county. That should be a lively conversation among the jurisdictions. I went back and began telling Bryan the good news. I pointed out the old concrete markers sticking up out of the pine straw in relation to the body. The conversation ended as General Custer arrived at the scene.

A large blonde man strode up with hints of grey in his hair and goatee. He talked loudly, said a lot, and didn't always make sense. He reminded me of the cartoon character of the oversized rooster that talked a lot, mostly spouting gibberish. The man probably went straight from high school bully to law enforcement. He dressed the part with long shank black polished boots and a tall white cowboy hat. An American Mounty, ready to swoop in and bust up an old ladies' card game. And look preposterous while doing it. I had no idea how he had gotten elected sheriff of Hamilton county. Maybe he didn't dress like an overgrown bantam rooster when he first campaigned for office. I noticed the only person paying attention to him was his deputy.

"Chief Wilson, thank you for securing my crime scene," Sheriff Jefferson Jackson said. "You can leave now. Take this civilian, whoever he is, with you."

"No," I said.

"Move along or I'll have you arrested." He finally bothered to look at me.

"No."

"I don't know who you are, but I'm going to have my deputy take you in for obstruction of a crime scene. Deputy Deacon, handcuff this idiot."

"No, that's not going to happen," Bryan said. "You are in my jurisdiction, so you will need to leave if you have nothing to contribute to the investigation. The consultant stays."

"I know you think you're a real lawman, but we all know you are just a bureaucratic appointment with a car that has blue lights. You need to shut up and get on or I'll arrest you as well."

"The border markers clearly show we are standing on city and park property," I said. "Look for yourself." He looked like he wanted to hit me and was on the verge of spewing something from his mouth. He did glance at the two points where I was pointing. His mouth closed, and he looked as if he had swallowed a lemon. His whole head turned bright red as the markers registered in his reptilian brain.

"Those idiots..." he said as he bit off the rest of whatever he intended to say. I assumed he meant us. He turned around and stomped off, with Deputy Deacon looking bewildered and then following him out of the woods.

"I don't think you made a good impression on Sheriff Jackson," Bryan said with a smile. "Anybody ever tell you that you might have a problem with authority?"

"Only every authority figure I ever knew. I guess General Custer won't be sending me a Christmas card."

CHAPTER FIVE

I saw Bryan at the cafeteria when I went over for breakfast. My breakfasts were faster than they used to be, as I had to get to the bookstore.

"Good morning Bryan."

"Ah, just the gentleman I wanted to see. Do you have time to talk today?"

"Sure. How about I come home for lunch and we do sandwiches and iced tea on the porch?"

"Sounds great. Around noon?"

"Yes, I'll be back from the store by then."

I left Kat in the shop before lunch. She would be fine for an hour. Lottie said she would check on her. That meant Kat would get a piece of chicken for a snack while

Lottie got to pet her. I pedaled home and got the sand-wiches ready just as Bryan appeared at the door. We ate before talking.

"This is good," Bryan said. "What is it?"

"Obviously not brisket like I fed you before," I said. "But I do a special marinade on turkey breast steaks. To me, it's nearly as good as brisket but different. I try to grill a batch a couple of times a year. Have fresh sandwiches for a few days then put the rest in the freezer."

"I would have guessed pork tenderloin. It does not taste like the turkey I know."

"Definitely not, but better. I'm guessing you need to know more about what I know about yesterday."

"Yes, I really do."

"Some of what you are about to ask me about is public information, and can be on the record. Some of it I'd rather not have on the record."

"I think your official background is all public. Tell me about the public record part first. I think I already know some of it."

"You do, after the last case. Basically, I know and can tell you a lot about the science of death and the aftermath of what happens to a body, but not from the standpoint of a coroner or a forensic scientist. Although I suppose we do similar research, but from very different perspectives. Along with that, I know a lot about death spasms, rigor mortis, body and muscle chemistry immediately after death, blood splash, determining the age of blood and bruises from their color, and dozens of other similar components of injury and death. It is animal-based, but humans are animals."

"And yet you've not done this on humans or worked with a coroner?"

"No, never. I've only worked with animals."

"I'm glad to know you know all that stuff. You could be valuable as a resource for a lot of violent crimes. On the other hand, I can't believe you know all that. That must have been some crazy kind of research."

"Most of it was mundane, actually. Only useful for improving the quality of meat. But that line of research completely wound down when corporations no longer cared about quality."

"OK, I get that. But that does not explain the other bits of knowledge you have about human torture and death. I'm guessing those were not research topics and not part of your public record."

"No, they were not. As you might imagine, there is a good explanation, but the details get a little touchy for some people. I assume you want the truth?"

"That would be best. Are you going to incriminate yourself?"

"No, I have not done those things. But you might be surprised that I know those that have. You might think less of me when I tell you about it."

"I doubt it. You seem straightforward and honest enough. Then again, some people said the same thing about Ted Bundy."

"I'm no Ted Bundy. But I have some skeletons in my closet. Namely, some family members. Have you heard of the Dixie Mafia?"

"I certainly have. They have faded a lot over the years but still run crime in some cities."

"You are right, they used to be much more obvious. But the dumb ones and the most obvious ones ended up in jail or dead. The ones that survived stayed quiet and away from the types of crime that garnered life sentences or the death penalty."

"Are you saying you are tied in to the survivors of the Dixie Mafia?"

"Very loosely. My family, on one side, has several members in the business."

"That must make for some interesting and explosive holiday gatherings."

"I would not know. I don't associate with them even for family events. Over the decades, I get a call every five or ten years, usually regarding a funeral after one of them dies."

"Then you don't work with them, for them, or have any contact?"

"As I said, the only ties are infrequent contacts. We don't do business and I'm not in the business. I made that decision as a teenager. I left town to attend college and never went back."

"Yet you know about beating toes to pulp and shooting someone in the thigh to get answers. And what powder burns look like from a gunshot."

"Before I left Atlanta for good, I was around that side of the family. Once I saw their business, I had to leave. It was barbaric to watch, which made my decision an easy one."

"That is good to know. For a time I thought you were either a criminal or vigilante. Well, maybe for a few seconds. From my cop's perspective, you don't seem the type."

"That is why they tried to recruit me. They figured I could get away with just about anything."

"That is somewhat less comforting. I don't think I'd like you as a criminal. You would have been quite successful I think."

"Maybe. But then I wouldn't be in a small town with a cat and a bookstore, trying to stay under the radar."

"Unless you were a brilliant criminal and looking for the perfect cover. Just kidding. Anyway, thanks for telling me. I feel better knowing about your background."

"Not going to charge me today? I don't ever use the crosswalk on the way to the cafeteria."

"Nah, I don't have room in my jail."

"You don't have a jail."

"There you have it, works out for both of us. Thanks for lunch. I have to get back and fill out another two hundred forms."

"Good luck."

After talking to Bryan, I walked around the campus, taking the outer loop. Millard's cottage was on the far lap and I saw he was home as I approached. The buggy was in the drive and I saw Millard on the porch swing. His hip must be feeling better, otherwise he'd have been in his chair. I had gotten to really like the old curmudgeon. He was probably one of the smartest people in town.

Lately I was able to take an occasional day off from the bookstore when I needed to. Millard was happy to come and watch the store and keep Kat company. It was good for him too. In bad weather, either George or I would take him to and from the store, where he had a comfortable chair surrounded by books. Otherwise he drove the "horseless buggy" to town, whether to Mable's or the bookstore. Easy enough since we were in the same building.

The first time he came to work at the store I was surprised by his change in persona. As each customer came in he would greet them, sometimes by name if they were older. If they asked him anything, he was gregarious and helpful. I saw the old Warm Springs mayor version of him. I noticed sales ticked up when he was there. Perhaps I needed to change my business model. Hire Millard and Kat, fire myself.

I also noticed there was often a plate under the counter. The same kind they used next door at Mable's. I guess he was getting fed on a regular basis. Maybe even having conversations, which were probably more important than food. Good for him. I always took the plate and slipped it on the bus cart without being obvious. If he and Lottie were keeping secrets, I'd let them. Besides, I knew Kat was making out like a bandit as well.

Occasionally I'd see a few elderly gentlemen going in and out of the store when Millard was working. I think Millard was setting up his old network again, from his mayoral days. I knew Lottie still had one going from her County Clerk days. Between the two of them, they probably did know where all the old skeletons lurked. They didn't do anything with social media, but I believed their network was more robust and fact-filled than anything online. I personally would take the immense knowledge base those two and their friends represented any day over ninety-five percent of what I could find on the internet.

The other outcome of his new venture was his weekly card game. I had not been invited yet. He told me he had four to eight regulars every week at his house. Games changed from pinochle and bridge to simple rummy and hardball poker. Apparently, poker games required each player to show up with one hundred dollars. You could play until broke. That sounded too rough for me.

"Hey Millard," I said as I got to his porch. The vest today was an understated silver paisley pattern.

"Hi James. Word is you have been deputized."

"Not really, just giving Bryan some observations."

"You should go into the business. It suits you."

"No thanks, I don't want to deal with criminals or bodies."

"Yet it seems to seek you out lately. Karma is knocking on your door."

"I'm just a lonely shopkeeper with a cat."

"Word is you aren't that lonely anymore."

"Gossip in this town is faster than the mail."

"Always has been, always will be. What do you think phones are for?"

"Mostly for sexting and internet surfing the videos from what I hear."

"Except for people my age. Neither of those pursuits is nearly as satisfying as gossip. It is what keeps us going."

"Maybe so. What is the latest gossip about me?"

"You made an impression on the young lady author, apparently."

"Yeah, destroying her signing event would do that."

"Oh, she doesn't blame you for that. Seems to like you for some reason, despite your attraction to the criminal element."

"I don't think she's heard about that. At least I have not mentioned it. Nor intend to."

"Don't worry. Give it a week and somebody will have given her your blood type and bank account numbers."

"I hope not. She'll find out how little money I have left. At least I'm asset-rich."

"Sure, hold on to that. We all know how that impresses the ladies. The old 'I have ten cows and fifty acres' pitch doesn't work that well anymore. Good thing she doesn't like you for your money."

"I don't know, we have not even had a date yet."

"Heard she's coming over Friday."

"She is supposed to. Don't you and Lottie come snooping by in the buggy."

"Would not dream of it. Nobody wants to do anything to mess it up. Hope you can do the same."

"I'll try not to. Does everybody already know what I'm wearing, or do they want to make suggestions? Or tell me what to cook?"

"Not yet. I'd say by Saturday afternoon we will have a critique ready for you, if you're interested."

"OK, enough about Donna. We can get into it next week when there might be something to talk about."

"There's always something to talk about. If not, we make something up. That is the beauty of the gossip chain."

"What is the latest on the body up on the ridge?"

"A lot of nonsense so far. Once the identity comes out, and if it's a local boy, the chain will kick into overdrive. We'll know everything, and make up what we don't."

"Sounds untrustworthy."

"It can be. But ever since the body last spring, the chain

has gotten a lot better and more active. It's a shame it happened, but it kickstarted the old network back into gear. We might even be of some help, depending on the identity of the deceased."

"I'll keep that in mind. But I don't know if Bryan will keep me around on the case."

"He will, that's for certain. You proved your bonafides last year. I bet you've already given him something he didn't know."

"Maybe, but he's a good investigator on his own."

"That's why we think you two will solve this quickly."

"Oh really? What does the betting pool say?"

"I can't tell you that. Although I have money on both twelve days and fourteen days. Lottie has ten and fifteen to cover her on both ends, plus an outer limit bet. All the other days are taken up to day twenty. Of course, the early day bettors are getting anxious. They should have known better as you can't get it solved that quick without a confession."

"You guys are really something."

"We are, but it works in your favor."

"How so?"

"We are running our own investigation, so to speak. Trying to find out everything we can."

"So you can game the system, then give me or Bryan the information and have it solved on one of the days you have bets on."

"Of course. Like I said, better than sexting or videos on the phone any day."

CHAPTER SIX

I had been thinking about my dinner with Donna. I was
nervous since I had not been on a date in a few years.
Actually, it was a few decades. But I didn't want to count
up just how long it had been. I kept telling myself it was
not a date. It was my way of apologizing for the book
signing incident. Besides, I was sure she didn't think my
asking her to dinner was a date either. Nah, of course not.
Two people went to eat together all the time without it
being a date. It sounded lame even to me. It also did not
relieve the nervousness.

Despite the events of the week, I decided not to talk to
Donna about the dead body. I wasn't ready to talk about it
yet, plus it would make for a macabre dinner conversation.

It would also likely to progress to the Tammy Wilkins murder, and the finale of the show, the murderer dying right here in the house. Unless she was made of stern and humorous stuff, it was not first date material.

I had dinner mostly prepared, from the salad to the roasted chicken. The wine was uncorked and sampled; it was good. The house was clean, and the yard looked fine. Everything was in shape. I even shaved, or rather removed all facial hair over a quarter-inch long.

The past few days I could not decide what to have for dessert. I considered a key lime pie, but today I had changed my mind. Instead, I was doing roasted and glazed persimmons, cooled and served with a honeyed mascarpone cream. I had them ready to go in the oven. I wanted them warm and fresh rather than cooking them ahead of time. Everything else would be cooked before she arrived, so we could spend more time talking while I finished up the details. I liked to cook and talk as long as the cooking wasn't too intense. The persimmons would be the opportunity for that.

I saw Donna pull in the drive. It was time to act natural and not do anything stupid. Not always a given with me. I opened the door for her and she came in with flowers. A nice touch, and I put them in a vase on the table. Kat immediately came over to meet her. Then she hung around and Donna scratched her neck and petted her back. Kat still highly approved, but she might be having flashbacks to pastries on the floor.

"Thanks for the flowers. Would you like wine before or during dinner?"

"Both? I can take a half glass now, if you don't mind."

"Sure. I'll pour us a light one and show you the house."

"Sounds great. I love old houses. I've lived around here for years and I've never been on campus. But since you live beside the police station it was easy to find. Campus is really something."

"Just imagine how it must have looked in the 1950s or 1960s. All the cottages and buildings were full of people. I'd bet campus was bigger than Warm Springs."

"I can see that. How did you find this cottage?"

"Mostly luck. I'd been watching real estate for a couple of years and just happened to see this listing a few minutes after it posted. I knew I wanted to live in a place that was easy to walk around and had amenities. Especially if it was a campus atmosphere."

"With your background you must have lived on a campus somewhere."

"No, never did. But I knew I would like it."

"The house is great. These look like original heart of pine floors."

"They are as far as I know. It has been remodeled more than once. Also, when I was working on the kitchen and removing an old cabinet I found seven different colors of paint on the old beadboard behind it. The original color was a dark army green. Although the varnished, unpainted wood likely was the original look for many years."

"Dark army green. I guess that was a fashion statement a long time ago. This is a big fireplace. Are you going to leave it as is?"

"I'm not sure. I can't tell if it is original or a remodel. The bricks and the broken red tile hearth make me think it is a remodel. But I can't decide what to do with it. Ive taken pictures of some fireplaces in other cottages and the Little White House. But every fireplace I've seen is different."

"Show me your bedroom. Time to see if you keep the other rooms as neat as the public spaces."

"Right through that door."

"Oh, the same floors. More importantly, still neat. Is that the bath?"

"Yes."

"Wow, this is a nice space. I was expecting something much smaller."

"I was surprised too. I believe it was also renovated some time ago. I'm sure they took space from under the stairwell to make the space larger."

"Interesting shower with the big window."

"That and the vanity are the only things I've changed in here. I did not want to give up the window, so it got incorporated into the shower."

I showed her the other bedroom and bath. Then we went upstairs to see the mini library. She seemed impressed with the house.

"This is nice. An old house still in good shape."

"Something us humans should strive for."

"I agree. I want to look this good at 100."

"I'd settle for looking good at 65. Anything past that will be a bonus. I need to finish up dessert, but everything else is ready. Would you like to talk in the kitchen?"

"Certainly. Oh my, this is a chopped-up space."

"Yes, I'm still trying to decide how to remodel. I want to keep the character but modernize. Maybe do something crazy like adding a dishwasher."

I finished the dessert then put the food on the table. We

sat in the dining room for dinner and more conversation. And another glass of wine, talking and eating.

"James, this is wonderful."

"Thanks. I'm glad you like it."

"What is your inspiration?"

"I like to cook, especially when I've had a great meal and try to recreate it in my own way. The main meal tonight was inspired by something I had in Paris."

"And the dessert?"

"A variation of something I've thought about for a while. I have always liked persimmons but couldn't think of a good way to serve them. I saw a recipe and changed it to fit my idea of a persimmon dish."

"Well, it is excellent. I've rarely had them, but these were great."

"Thanks. I do them for breakfast as well."

"Is that an invitation?"

My mind stopped for a second. Possibly my mouth was open. She began laughing. "James, you should see yourself. Just like a deer on the highway in headlights."

I laughed too. "You had me there for a second. The next meal was about to be venison. You know, the one that got hit on the road."

"So, you are asking me to dinner again?"

I was ready this time. "I am. But only if you like roadkill."

"Wonderful. If you keep cooking like this, I'll move in next month. Even roadkill."

"I'll have to check with Kat first."

"Oh, she'll be fine with it."

"If not, she bribes easily, like pastries on the floor. Mainly snacks and belly rubs are her currency."

"Those tend to work for me too."

"Oh," was all I had to say, as Donna burst out laughing.

"James, I'm just kidding. I have slightly higher standards for a first date. A nice dinner and a spa day with a massage for a minimum."

"I can provide dinner, but fresh out of spas. But I do have a sauna."

"You do? Where is it at?"

"Out back by the basement door. I custom built it because I could not find anything I liked for sale."

"How large is it?"

"It will fit two comfortably."

"Thinking ahead I see."

"More like I wanted room to fall over if I passed out."

"You say the most romantic things."

"Your sarcasm is noted and seconded by many people. I could never keep up with a romance author, anyway."

"I bet you could."

"I doubt it. I'm really not good at speaking or writing whatever language romance uses. But I suppose you get plenty of practice writing for characters."

"I do. But you should know my teasing is just that, a way of using words for surprise. I find it fun, but I have to be careful not to go too far. I'd have to get to know you much better before I'd be tempted to follow up with any of my teasing."

"That is fine with me. I would have a difficult time starting anything with someone I did not know well."

"Oh, come on, I bet you woo the women and have them stay over."

"I'm telling on myself, but I've never had a one-night stand."

"Really, never? That is hard to believe."

"But true. I don't know, it just never happened. Probably because I didn't try very hard. I do think I need to know someone first."

"Well, that is good to know. I won't seduce you on our first date."

"I'm so relieved to hear that. Being seduced is so scary."

"Now you are teasing me."

"I sure am. But it is good to talk openly and not have to fret about you taking me seriously or trying to seduce you."

"That is nice. We have plenty of time for seductions in the future."

"How long have you been living in the area?" I decided it was time to change subjects.

"I had been coming down from Atlanta for years and visiting Pine Gardens. Then, about fifteen years ago my husband and I bought a small house down here. We fixed it up for weekends and vacation. I asked for it and got it in the divorce, and he kept the big house in Dunwoody."

"Oh, posh Atlanta."

"They can have it. It was a nice house, but too many people and cars. Noisy all the time and no chance of seeing the night sky."

"I know what you mean. I don't think any amount of money could get me to live there. How did you start writing?"

"I like writing, so I decided to try to go from hobby to

commercial. Imagining all the characters and how they meet, fall in love, then deal with all the obstacles. It's like play acting my own life, but I get to have more direction in what happens. I also make a decent living at it. But the part I don't like is having to put out a set number of books per year to maintain that income."

"I understand. I don't make much income but I don't need to, fortunately. Historical fiction isn't a moneymaking genre like romance can be. I like writing and sometimes use it as therapy."

"That makes sense. Working on character development maybe makes me more aware of what is happening in my own life. Why did you choose historical fiction?"

"I've lived long enough to observe firsthand how a major event happened or what a person did. Then I read or hear about it thirty years later, and it is a very different account from what I knew. It is usually written by someone too young to have been a real-time observer. Or maybe it was written by a partisan selling a certain ideology."

"Yes, I can think of a few instances where I have noticed that."

"So, if other people make stuff up about what really happened, then I can too. But from the perspective of making it more interesting. At least I hope so. Plus, history keeps evolving. A hundred years ago, nobody believed the Vikings found North America long before Columbus. Now it is a fact they did. But we don't know much about those people. That gives me latitude to make thing up, based on the archaeological evidence but mostly on what I know about people and their behavior."

"I do the same thing, but most of my writing is in the present. Modeling the character's behavior on what I know and understand about human desires, motives, and the actions that come from those basic needs and wants."

"And what does Donna want?"

"That's a loaded question. Probably what everyone wants. A peaceful life, secure, with good friends and good health."

"Those are excellent wants. I second all those, plus I have to add in travel."

We finished dinner, and afterwards, Donna, Kat, and I walked around the yard. I took the opportunity to show her the sauna and the guest cottage. She, like me, saw the potential in the guest cottage. Assuming of course, that I ever finished it. We went back inside as it was getting dark. She left, but we shared a kiss first. My first date in many years was over and apparently successful. The rest of the evening, I spent with Kat in my chair.

CHAPTER SEVEN

The day began sunny and warm. I was up early on a Saturday to get to the bookstore and catch any weekend book buyers. Since I was the only book monger in town, maybe I'd make some sales. Kat was coerced into the carrier, we got on the bike and off we went to town. We arrived in about four minutes. I gave Kat her promised snack, then she went to bathe in the window. She was my best "open" sign.

I had more customers than expected. Sold a few books and took two orders. At this rate, I could retire again in 2053. Lottie came over to give Kat a snack, but since I had people walking around and Mable's was getting busy, we did not have a chance to either kid each other or talk business. Not long after lunch, when my traffic slowed down, I put Kat back on the bike and put the closed sign on the door. I might lose a couple of sales, but it was barely worth the time spent waiting. Food for the week was waiting for me to prepare and cook it.

Kat left the carrier and zoomed outside. She had chipmunk duty for the next two hours. Meanwhile, I took two chickens, both cut in half, and roasted them on the grill. I got four portions of white meat and Kat got the dark meat, her favorite. We were obviously meant to live in the same house. Since the grill was hot I added sliced zucchini, yellow squash, mushrooms and asparagus. Between those and a few fresh tomatoes, I had my vegetables and protein for the week. I cut up fresh fruit drenched in my lemon juice-powdered sugar slurry to keep it from browning during the week. Everything got bagged up and put in the refrigerator and I was done for the week.

I sent Donna a text, and we had a non-verbal conversation while I sat on the front porch and supervised Kat. If Kat knew I was there, she did not seem to mind. Eventually she came back to the porch for some neck and face scratching. Then she was off to the backyard to prowl or possibly take a nap. I invited Donna to go hiking the next day, but she had an editing deadline to meet. I understood that burden and wished her well.

The evening would be slow, so I thought about going over the new murder case. Or I could work on the old murder case from decades ago. My decision was neither. It would be an iced tea evening with music, just me and Kat.

We ate, then I walked around campus, just the quad tonight, a few times. Back in my chair with tea and Kat, reading up on some new science fiction. Not a bad day and evening.

Sunday morning was sunny and breezy, but not enough to need a coat. I made my way across campus and along the extensive dam of the man-made lake. The same lake where I had noticed Tammy Wilkins' body the previous spring. I was still glad I had not seen the body up close. Not that I had hadn't seen many bodies, because I had, but not of humans. Hers was a senseless murder by her realtor partner over money. It was a lot of money, but still, an idiotic reason to end another's life.

I walked on into the woods and through the groundskeeper's graveyard. No human bodies here, just lots of worn out equipment parked in a young cutover forest. A tractor, a few large mowers, a seeder, trailers, and a few things I could not identify. All had given their lives to maintain the large campus and now rested and rusted away, safely out of sight from anyone but a few. Pushing past, I entered heavier and older woods. The old logging road was rutted and eventually filled with water from an old spring seep a hundred yards uphill. My waterproof boots kept my feet dry.

I arrived at the creek I needed to cross in order to access the official trail. A loop of the Pine Mountain Trail descended the ridge and ran parallel to campus for a bit. I jumped the creek to get on the trail and began ascending Pine Mountain proper. The campus sat on a knoll of the ridge network, but now I was going up on the main ridge.

Pine straw and leaves were being pushed aside as spring shoots were popping up everywhere. Some were welcome native shoots and flowers. Unfortunately, one of those natives was poison ivy. Most years I never had a problem with it. I wasn't sure if my immune system was sporadic or if some plants had more concentrated or a different composition of urushiol than others. Better to not research those questions with my skin and just stay away from it.

Despite it being a nice Sunday, I didn't encounter other hikers. The trail more or less followed Cascade Branch upstream, eventually to Cascade Falls. Along the way, I went through longleaf pine stands and mountain laurel thickets. Two species that ought not exist together, but this was a special ecological niche, blending Appalachian mountain species with Piedmont and Coastal Plain species. I sat for a few minutes on rock ledges along a barren ridge butting from the forest. The view over the creek and the variety of foliage was pleasant and the breeze welcome after the hike so far. Not much farther I came to the main attraction of the trail, Cascade Falls.

A few people were there since it was easily reached by the trail coming down from the main road along the top of Pine Mountain. I did not stay long and kept uphill to the road, then along it to the parcels once scheduled to be cleared for a massive development. The same one Tammy was killed over. The survey markers remained, but the orange ribbons and paint were fading in the Georgia sun. As far as I knew, the project was under consideration but frozen while a real environmental assessment was under-way. One which might well kill the project. As with many such projects, those placed to profit from them were outspoken about pushing forward. I had intervened by anonymously sending a private study showing negative consequences of the project to organizations that subsequently sued to prevent it. I'd gotten the secret study from Joe Burrow's house after he tried to kill me. Those pushing for the development suspected my involvement, and I was not popular in certain crowds. A position I had found myself in many times, so I was comfortable enough.

I began descending the ridge back to campus. I let my mind wander back to the body found on Friday. Someone went to much effort to extract something from the victim. I knew people in Atlanta that practiced the same type of coercive methods. But I would not contact them yet. Hopefully not at all, but certainly not without more information regarding the case. Those methods were not restricted to the Atlanta branch of the Dixie Mafia.

I truly hoped this was going to be unlike my last, and only, murder investigation. I did not want to end up with a gun in my face in my own house. Nor having that person's dead body on my living room floor moments later. He could have stained my floor and rug with the poisoned whiskey. That would have been impolite.

I thought less about it the farther I walked. There was too little information thus far to continue thinking about the murder. Since Bryan was leading the investigation this time, he should have access to the resources the state investigators had to offer. Sometimes I thought those resources were more valuable than the investigators themselves. The next few days, I was sure we would have more information to work with.

My mind was freer to enjoy the hike back. I began

noticing all the new growth bursting out of the brown forest floor. Some even had tiny flowers. The moss along the old road bank was also looking lush. A few patches had rising stalks with tiny heads. I called them spore stalks, but from an old class I think they were actually seta. The woods were loud today from bird activity. Mating and nesting were well underway and all the feathered creatures, at least the males, were stridently marking their territory.

This might be my last hike on this route for the season. The warm weather was nice, but the bugs, especially ticks, along with poison ivy and snakes, were also appreciative of and thriving in the weather. I could drive up to the top of Pine Mountain and take the established trail from there downhill without traipsing through the woods. It took the spontaneity out of walking from my house, but was definitely safer. Once the first frost came in the fall, I could resume.

I left the woods and came to the lake. I thought about how lucky I had been to find this place and settle here. Or maybe it was due to being in the right place and time after making smart preparations. Most of my life I thought I'd rather be lucky than good. If I was good, then there could always be someone better; but when my luck was running hot, there was no one luckier than me. But I'd rather be lucky and good most days to cover all bases. Being good got me to the point of figuring out that Joe had killed Tammy; being lucky got him to drink poisoned whiskey before he shot me in the head.

I got back to Kat, and she showed her joy by ignoring

me. She only did it ten times a day. Washing clothes was my next weekend adventure. I was living the life now. But all things considered, I was content in my cozy home in a campus niche. Tomorrow I would go out into the world and realize how lucky I was all over again.

CHAPTER EIGHT

I took two minutes and walked over to Bryan's office. Might as well start off Monday morning right.

"Hey Bryan."

"James, what a pleasure."

"Seriously? I'm usually bringing bad news or more work."

"Yes, you do. But you make life in the campus police department so much more interesting."

"I'm glad you are so optimistic."

"Not exactly optimistic. More like exciting with the strong chance of a bad ending."

"Like a speeding car on icy roads?"

"That is a perfect description."

"What am I here for? Insults thrown at my winter driving ability?"

"You started that topic. But no, I intended to update you on the case."

"Go ahead if that will stop these egregious attacks on my character."

"Yeah, right. Anyway, the body was identified as Mike Vickers. Last known address was Peachtree City. Here, take a look at these photos." There were three color photographs showing a closeup of different tattoos. "Do you recognize any of these?"

"No. Something about them reminds me of military ink. But I'm more familiar with the old tattoos from WWII or Vietnam that I've seen on older family. I have not seen much from all the newer activity in the Middle East."

"We thought the same thing. One of our guys knew about this one. We sent the other two off and expect confirmation shortly. Meanwhile, we confirmed the victim was in the military. He flew transport planes during three tours overseas."

"Any idea how he ended up in Warm Springs, laying out there on Pine Mountain?"

"He had family in the area, but no, the reason for his presence so far is unknown."

"What is the preliminary from the coroner?"

"About what you already know. Gunshot wound to the leg, nonfatal. Trauma to the toes on the left foot, nonfatal. Two gunshot wounds to the chest from a 9mm, very fatal. Coroner estimates the leg and toes were injured approximately two hours before the fatal shots. Now, tell me what you know about the thigh shot and the toes. Considering what we talked about last week."

"He was obviously tortured. Not sure why, of course. The upper leg has a lot of soft tissue. Passing a high-speed bullet through it causes a lot of pain and misery. Completely recoverable if you don't hit the bone or artery. But miss the angle and hit the bone and bad things happen. A busted femur means the victim really can't recover enough to talk much afterward. Clip the artery and the victim bleeds out in one minute. It is a shot that needs practice.

"The toes are self-explanatory. Watch a bad gangster movie and you'll see it done. Again, a lot of pain without permanent injury. Although the toes, if bad enough, might have had to be amputated. You only do this to someone if you really don't like them, or if you need something from them. Or need them to do something."

"All of that makes sense. It was probably a mob hit."

"Not necessarily. There is the possibility it was staged to look like a mob hit."

"But most regular folks would not know about the torture options."

"I hope not. But one group that knows includes the police."

"You think law enforcement personnel were involved?"

"No idea, but some on the force would know about those methods. At least in Atlanta, you would have to list the police as a possibility. Down here, it seems unlikely."

"I hope so, because I don't like those implications. What about the two-hour delay between the initial wounds and death?"

"Could be lots of reasons. They had to check on something he told them. They had to take him somewhere and check his story. Or the boss was late giving the kill order."

"That's about what we think so far."

"Are you keeping the case or is the state taking over?"

"There has been some contention. The county sheriff is all worked up, but he can't get jurisdiction, no matter how much he squeals. The state has backed off, probably because of how they botched the Tammy Wilkins case. Not to mention completely missing Joe as a suspect until he was dead."

"Because they value and trust you implicitly or they are waiting for you to screw up?"

"I think we both know it is the latter. That is why we will solve this thing and tie it up nice and tidy. You are no longer an unofficial consultant."

"Thanks, I can go back to my bookstore."

"Oh no, you are now an official consultant. You get paid expenses and everything."

"There probably won't be any expenses."

"See how that works for us."

"Do I get a badge and gun?"

"Of course not. But you can requisition business cards."

"How long will those take?"

"Request now, and the approval process will go through in approximately thirty days. Fifty percent chance it will be approved on the first pass. After approval, the printing and delivery will take 90 to 180 days. Start now and you might be official by the end of the year."

"Can I get a blue light for the bicycle?"

"Feel free to purchase what you think you might need.

We can reimburse you. Reimbursements usually come back from the county in 90 days. Oh, five dollars a day is your limit."

"I'm beginning to see the downside to being an official consultant."

"You can put it on your resume."

"That would be impressive if I weren't a retired book-store owner with no plans to ever apply for another job."

"If we gave out perks anyone would want the job."

"OK, enough with the stellar benefits. What's the plan? How can I help?"

"Locate where he was killed. Find out why he was killed. Locate the murder weapon. Apprehend the killer."

"Oh, I thought it was going to be hard. I can do all that by tomorrow."

"That's why you are an official consultant. But right now, can you check into his job or business interests? Doing that probably won't require police assistance. We have preliminary information, but you have a knack for finding the ugly details. But if you run into anything odd or someone threatening, call me immediately. Walk away and don't take any chances."

"I can do that. Give me his full name, address, driver's license number, or anything else you have so far."

"Edna has the file on her desk. Good luck. And remember, no conflicts or craziness. Just information. If anyone gets out of line, let us know and we will handle it. If you find anything of major importance, please call me. Otherwise, let's meet back in a couple of days."

I walked the hundred feet to my house with Edna's file. I sat on the porch and reviewed the few pages inside. There was not much to answer my lines of investigation, but it was a start. I came up with a brief summary. Vickers was associated with aviation. Although Bryan had not confirmed it, I suspected he maintained a pilot's license. Somehow, he had money to live in Peachtree City. He must have had something somebody else wanted, therefore the torture. The logical conclusion was that Vickers was involved with something criminal.

What should I focus on first? I decided I needed three lines of information. First, to find out who Mike Vickers was. Second, to find out what he did. And last, why he was in Warm Springs. That should also keep me away from Bryan's more in-depth investigation. The white boards went back up in the study upstairs.

Mike Vickers was originally from Atlanta. After a few years of menial jobs, he went to the Middle East for three tours of duty. Came back and had a spotty work history. He seemed to drift in and out of aviation-type jobs. Worked at two smaller airports in Georgia. Applied to be an air traffic controller but didn't make it past the final evaluations. Those were likely to be the detailed background check or the psychological evaluation, or both. Lately he was with a private company I had never heard of. I assumed it was something to do with airports, but I would research the company later. He appeared to be a former pilot that wanted to get back to flying, yet something kept him from it. I made a note to check if he had a current pilot's license in case Bryan did not.

The information so far, plus what I had noted for later research should help with the first two lines of inquiry. Now I needed to know why he was here. I went into research mode. Bryan said he had family in the area, so I looked at Vickers' former addresses and property records, and for his parent's names and his mother's maiden name. I started cross-referencing names with Hamilton County property records. I knew once I did all I could on the computer, I'd be paying Mable's Diner a visit to talk to Lottie. As the former County Clerk and overall knower of everything, I was sure she could help.

From what I found, Vickers' family on one side was from Hamilton County. In fact, just outside the city limits of Warm Springs. Going west in the direction of the town of Pine Mountain, about two miles out. I made a note of associated addresses and would drive out to see the land and houses for myself. There were several small plots with houses near the road. Several large parcels of land behind them, mostly wooded. There was a lake on one of the parcels. Viewing the satellite map, I switched to the elevation mode. The lake was unusual in that it had very steep banks. Probably not a family fishing lake.

I was getting bored, so I got in the car and drove out to the area I had just perused online. Driveways came into view along the highway when I neared the addresses associated with Vickers' family. Some of the houses I could see from the road and they looked normal. Some were too far back to see. It was wooded, but the trees looked older and worn. Reminded me of the way trees grew in Arkansas in the mountains. The dirt along the road was more of a red-orange color that also reminded me of Arkansas dirt. Usually the dirt in this part of Georgia was a sandy off-white or the famous red clay. I could not see far through the woods, so the large lake was not visible. I turned around and drove back to Warm Springs.

I parked along the main drag not far from Mable's Diner and my bookstore. I had not brought Kat, as I didn't intend to stay long. I was closed Monday like more than half the businesses in town. The tourist season would begin soon, and I needed to rethink my open days and times.

I sat at the counter inside Mable's. Lottie brought me iced tea.

"Well now Romeo, you have been busy."

"Oh? What have you heard?"

"You cooked Donna a nice dinner and gave her the gentleman treatment. And you got a new job working with the police. All official, unlike last time."

"I'm only doing it for the money."

"The Campus Police Department don't pay consultants."

"I guess they will get what they pay for."

She made a face. "We both know you'd do it for free anyway. You crave adventure and seek mayhem."

"I like that. I think I'll adopt it as my new motto. Maybe have it stenciled across the side of my bicycle."

"Sure you will. What you having today?"

"The vegetable plate."

"You are going to regret that if you get run over by a truck after you eat. Knowing you could have had the special of a bratwurst with cheese, chili, onions and slaw."

"It would have the same effect as the truck, just slower as my arteries clog shut."

"Veggies it is. Can't believe you want to live forever."

"Not forever, just longer than average."

Lottie left to deliver the order and deal with other customers. I would wait until the lunch rush left before asking Lottie about my new project. I watched people come and go, mostly go since lunch was ending, in the mirror that went part way across the back wall behind the counter. A few were familiar, but most were not. I had not been living in town long enough to know all the customers by name like some did.

Lottie came back and brought my food, refilled my tea, and hurried on to get tickets to departing diners. Ten minutes later she was across from me on the other side of the counter.

"I get the feeling you are hanging around and waiting for me. I'll tell you now I'm not romantically available, so you look elsewhere."

"Lottie, as appealing as that scenario is, I'm not seeking your company in a romantic way."

"Good, now that is settled what are you wanting? Are we talking about Donna or the dead body?"

"The body. His name was Mike Vickers. Supposed to have had family here, just west of town."

"I know some of the folks, mostly from courthouse dealings and such. I did not know Mike, but the name sounds familiar."

"I believe he was from Atlanta, most recently lived in Peachtree City."

"OK, now I remember. His parents were from hereabouts. They moved to Atlanta after they got married. Must have had their kids up there."

"Sounds right. You probably don't know the parents or the son then."

"Just the parents when they were young."

"Anything you remember that might have brought Mike back here? Maybe they came back after they retired?"

"I don't think so. But I can find out easy enough. You gonna be in your store tomorrow?"

"That is my intention. I have big plans to get rich."

"Then you must have a counterfeit money operation going on over there."

"Something like that."

"Sure you don't want to talk about Donna?"

"Nah, I'm good. If you have any good gossip though, you can tell me tomorrow."

"Sure will."

CHAPTER NINE

Kat and I took the bicycle transit route to the bookstore Tuesday morning. I kept the bike inside just in case a local Warm Springs bikejacker decided to take a joy ride on a rigged-out Dutch transport bike. Most people probably would not want to be seen on such a thing, but I thought it was incredibly useful. Yet even I thought it was on the clunky and ugly scale compared to sleek road bikes, or even electric bikes. I was not ready for an ebike but knew there could be a day when my knees were worn out requiring I get one.

I brought lunch for Kat and I and we ate with music on the portable speaker I carried. The morning was slow, with only a few customers and one that picked up an ordered book. When the lunch rush diminished, I went next door to Mable's. I sat in a booth rather than the counter. I ordered strawberry pie from Lottie, as the berries were coming in fresh right now. She brought the pie and iced tea and I was entranced for a few minutes. As the rest of the customers filtered out, Lottie came and sat across from me with her glass of tea.

"You inhaled that right quick. Don't remember you liking strawberry pie."

"I get it once or twice a year, right when the berries come in for the season. Seemed like a good idea today."

"Those were fresh berries. Another six weeks and they won't be. Now let's talk about Donna."

"That wasn't my first choice, but why not?"

"From what I've heard it went well. You were nice to her. Didn't say anything stupid. Gave her a nice dinner and dessert. You are going to have to tell me about the persimmons. Never had them like that and might have to add them to the menu. Could be a fall special."

"Are you going to name the dish after me?"

"I will. Something like Wilder's Persimmons."

"You might need to get more creative."

"Definitely. Maybe Jim's Persimms. Now, back to the main topic. When are you going to ask her out again?"

"Soon I think. We've traded texts, and I called her last night."

"Good, keep staying in the game."

"Thinking of asking her to Pine Gardens this weekend. Walk around and see the tulips and azaleas. I'm trying to decide whether or not to eat there."

"There are a few places around there. Most are average. Why not be original and take a picnic?"

"Excellent idea, Lottie."

"Don't sound so surprised. Now that we've got your personal life on track, time to work on your professional development."

"Ugh, that phrase brings up bad memories of the corporate world. What have you got on Mike Vickers?"

"You know some of the basics. Does have family still around, while the parents lived in and raised him in Atlanta. They visited down here on holidays and went to Pine Gardens some summers. His dad, being on the Vickers side, seemed to have issues with some of his kin. Their visits got fewer over the years. Then it got worse. The old matriarch of the whole brood died and left the big piece of land off the highway to Mike's dad. Doyle Vickers, who would be Mike's father's first cousin, did not like that one bit. Threatened Mike's parents a few times, and even had to get the sheriff involved when he pulled a gun on them. I'll tell you about Doyle sometime."

"Anything particularly valuable or noteworthy about the land?"

"Not really. I think it was more about it being in the family for generations. The local bunch believed that going off to Atlanta to live was a betrayal and relieved one of the right to being a real Vickers."

"Enough bad blood to shoot Mike over it? Doesn't seem like it since Mike's dad owned it."

"Not anymore he don't. The father passed ten years ago, and his mother just died and left it to Mike last year."

"Did he sell it already? That might be how he could afford Peachtree City life."

"No, he didn't. He must have won the lottery to live up there. But back to Doyle. It is possible he's hotheaded enough to do something like that."

"The name sounds familiar, but I can't place it."

"He has a towing business in the county. You might have seen his trucks around the area. He keeps a bunch of junk cars around his place, making his neighbors, all family, mad at him. Probably does it on purpose."

"I drove out there but didn't see anything from the road."

"He lives back off the road in the woods. Not far from the lake."

"Makes sense. I could not see the lake either. Guess he wanted it for fishing."

"Probably not, as I don't think much lives in that lake."

"Why is that?"

"It is part of an old mine. Gouged out of the ground to get minerals years before I was born. Water filled it in but don't think its fit for much."

"Maybe there is still something there worth killing for. Some kind of valuable mineral."

"I doubt it. Whatever they got out of it, it closed down more than a hundred years ago."

"I thought you said it was years before you were born?"

"Cracks like that will get your pie quota restricted. As in none."

"Yeah, the mine angle sounds like a dead end. Anybody know why Mike was down here recently?"

"No, but it wasn't to visit family. Doyle is so ornery he

would have run him off on sight. Mike's car was seen around a few times. He might have been on his way to Columbus. Supposed to have a girlfriend or friend down there. Some service buddies still on the base or nearby, previously in the service."

"What kind of car did he have?"

"One of those new muscle cars. Mustang or Charger, something like that. Bright red and loud."

"I'll also ask Bryan about the car. Anything else interesting?"

"No, but people have just started talking. This next week, all manner of things are likely to pop up. Even though ninety percent will be fake."

"Well, thanks for this, and let me know what else comes up."

"I shall. Do you need a bag for Kat?"

"I already fed her lunch."

"I'll pack something for her afternoon snack. Now you get to thinking about what to make Donna for your picnic."

"Yes ma'am."

Returning to the store, I was greeted by Kat. She knew I was bringing a treat from Mable's. She ate her hamburger with gusto. I only fed her chicken or other poultry and she appreciated an occasional red meat snack. Soon enough, Kat would revolt and install Lottie as her new human servant.

I thought about Vickers, but not for long. His family situation sounded volatile and I would need to look into it. I assumed Bryan might already be doing that, so I moved on to the more important assignment that Lottie gave me.

My initial thought was to eat at Pine Gardens or a

restaurant in Pine Mountain. Lottie's idea of a picnic was more appealing. But I did not know Donna well enough to know what she might like in a picnic basket. I did something rarely done in America—I called her.

"Hello James."

"Hi Donna. Are you busy?"

"Not really, just writing. Time for a break anyway. My main character wants to go back to her old boyfriend but the new guy is the right one for her."

"You should have a talk with her."

"I try. She doesn't listen sometimes."

"She must be part cat."

"Now that would be the worst entity ever. Part human and part cat. They would alternate between begging for food, ignoring you, then licking their arms when you tried to talk to them."

"That would be both annoying and distracting."

"Yes, but we probably have other things to talk about. What's going on?"

"I was thinking about us going to Pine Gardens this weekend, like I mentioned before. But instead of eating there, what do you think about taking a picnic meal instead?"

"That is a wonderful idea if you are bringing it. If you are leaving it to me, we can try the vending machine in the gas station instead."

"Oh, let's not do that. I'm calling to ask what you might want."

"Let me think. Nothing that will make me violently ill. And no peanut butter and jelly."

"I can guarantee you won't get sick. Do you have a peanut allergy?"

"Oh no, just sick of peanut butter and jelly sandwiches."

"But you never had one of mine."

"What makes yours so special?"

"I mix lime juice, cinnamon and honey with the peanut butter, then stir in the jelly, usually strawberry. Slap that on a slice of nice bread, then top with very thinly sliced cantaloupe. Makes a nice bite."

"I don't even know what to say. It is incredibly genius or the worst thing ever."

"Could be both, but I like it. But I will not bring it on our picnic. Maybe someday I'll serve it and you can decide between genius and nightmare modes."

"So what are you making?"

"I don't know yet. Something simple, safe, good, and non-leaky."

"That is what I wish my plumber was."

"Hopefully the food will be better than your plumber."

"I'll leave the food choices to you. Ply me with food and wine and I'm yours."

"Whatever would I do with you?"

"You will have to use your imagination. Oh, do you play golf?"

"I have before and was supposed to start again. One reason to move down here. Do you play?"

"Not much anymore. I played for my college team and I'd like to start again."

"Then I am likely not in your league. If we play, you'll have to give me a few strokes per nine holes." I heard nothing but laughter over the phone. "OK, that might have come across as poorly worded. But really, I'll have to watch myself around you. Never thought I'd have to clean up my golf language."

"Let's do the picnic. We can talk about a golf outing then. I'd like to walk nine holes at the end of a weekday when other players aren't rushing me."

"I feel the same way. If the picnic food does not kill you, we will schedule a day to go golfing."

"It's a deal."

CHAPTER TEN

The first thing the next morning Bryan came over even before I could get to the cafeteria. I opened the door before he knocked.

"Good morning Bryan."

"Hello James. I was trying to catch you before you left for the store."

"You are early. Even before my cafeteria trip."

"Sorry, I know we both have things to do today. Do you have five minutes?"

"Sure. As your official consultant, I deem you worthy."

"Thanks. Since last we talked, we have gotten more information about what Mike Vickers was doing lately. Apparently, he had been getting into the pot business."

"Which part? Using, buying, selling or smuggling it?"

"Bringing it in and possibly selling it. Our sources were not exactly clear. But we will have more information quickly now that we are focused on that aspect of his activities."

"Do you think that is why he was killed?"

"Not sure yet. The pot business is not as violent as much of the other, harder drugs. But big money in any illegal activity can cause problems. Sometimes people are killed in the pot business."

"How does the business work these days? I only remember years ago when a few people grew pot up in north Georgia. Also, it was brought in from Mexico or South America."

"There are more sources than before, plus different types of sources. Some pot is still imported from outside the US. Some still grown illegally for harvest and sale. What we've seen more of lately are smugglers importing it from legal states and distributing it in states where it is still illegal."

"Like in Georgia. Then it's brought in here from a legal state like Colorado. But if they are buying it there, they must be buying a lot at wholesale or deeply discounted prices. But then the suppliers must know that the quantities being bought mean it goes somewhere that it is not legal."

"Of course, but they don't ask questions, just like any good salesperson. We think some of the largest legal growers are pushing their excess crops at lower prices to the buyers from illegal states. They may be even growing more than their allotment, which is illegal, to fill the pipeline."

"But even though the pot might be legal most of the time, transporting the pot across state lines is still illegal."

"Yes, but minor amounts are rarely caught and taken to trial."

"Yet even in the states where legalized, pot is still illegal on the federal level."

"True, but the federal agencies have not been pursuing prosecutions in the legalized states. There are financial issues affecting the growers, like not being able to get bank loans, which pushes it into a mostly cash business. The practical matter of enforcing federal laws on pot crossing state lines falls into a lower priority at low volumes. But when it is a van load of pot sent to a state where it is still illegal, there is little grey area. Federal, state and local law enforcement takes action."

"Yeah, I understand an elderly person with health issues can get away with carrying a tea bag's amount of pot even in an illegal state, but a planeload or truckload is always going to be a problem."

"We will aggressively pursue charges for that quantity based on state law."

"You have evidence Mike Vickers' was involved at that level."

"Correct."

"What have your sources said about the activity happening in Hamilton County?"

"Large bulk quantities are brought in various ways and repacked into small units for sale. It is distributed out across the Southeast, and the cash comes back here."

"OK, Bryan, I could use general pot industry financial information. Both the legal side as well as the illegal."

"What are you thinking?"

"Follow the money. But to do that I need to know what places to look at here in Hamilton County."

"I can try to find somebody to get you that information."

"Thanks."

"I've used up five minutes and then some. I appreciate your valuable time, so please send me a bill. As long as it is not more than a dollar."

"I will. That should get me a pack of sugar for my coffee."

"See you later."

I did a fast trip to the cafeteria and then to the store. I took the bike since it was much faster than walking. Kat was in the carrier crate on the back. Although it was only a few hundred yards along the main street once off campus, I realized how vulnerable we were on a bike. An accident would be easy to arrange as a hit-and-run. Maybe I would start driving the car for the next couple of weeks if the pot people turned out to be dangerous.

Once at the store, Kat walked through the store rubbing her face on all her favorite corners. She swished her way back to the front to take her place in the window. She did not actually make a swishing sound. It was in my mind, watching her walk, carrying her massive fluff. I worked on a pile of papers I had been neglecting on purpose. Inventory, sales, upcoming releases, taxes. All the reasons that made bookstore ownership worth the investment. On the other hand, it had gotten me a date with

Donna. And I still enjoyed sitting here looking at and smelling all the books.

I also had time at the store to think since it was another slow morning. Mike Vickers living in Peachtree City made sense since he liked to hang around airports and the aviation crowd. Many people associated with the Atlanta airport lived in Peachtree City. What did not make sense in Vickers' case was that living there was expensive. Mostly, the residents were commercial airline pilots and airport administrators, not regular staff or flight attendants. His spotty employment record did not equate him to be a Peachtree City resident. I did not understand how Vickers could afford it unless he was living with someone. Of course, if he was in the pot business, then it made more sense. Depending on how deeply involved he was, he could afford the lifestyle.

I needed to drive up and check the address since it was less than an hour away. The value of Vickers' house would be a good indicator of his potential criminal activity. I could check the county records, but I really wanted to see it for myself. Besides, on the same trip, I could stop at the Georgia Archives to do some research on my old letter. It was in south Atlanta near Clayton State University.

Later, I heard a familiar engine buzzing into town. It stopped out front. I walked over to the door and watched Millard rise from the almost street-legal contraption I had given him. He slowly stepped up on the sidewalk, favoring his bad hip. I expected him to go next door to Mable's, but he came to my door. The vest of the day was sky blue, with several large scarlet dragons.

"Hey Millard. You celebrating your Welsh roots?" I

asked as I opened the door. Kat looked up from her nap but dropped her head, having sniffed no snacks.

"Good day James. Ah, you refer to my magnificent embroidered dragon friends. I have people that came from Wales. But this was a gift from a dear friend in China."

"I wondered where you got all those vests."

"I have a source in the UK I've been using for years. Since then, some of my friends began buying them for me occasionally."

"You must have a year's worth of them."

"I can go more than two months without a repeat."

"You probably did not stop by to discuss waistcoats. I'm keeping you from lunch."

"Lunch can wait a little longer. But I came by for a reason."

"What do you have, Millard?"

"I mentioned a while back about our group. I'm letting you know we are getting organized and ramping up for action."

"Are you guys going to start a neighborhood watch?"

"Not in the physical sense. We are all around eighty years old. Watching and listening is mostly what we do. But we have superpowers."

"Oh, what are they?" I pictured the octogenarians flying around with capes.

"First, we are invisible. Few people even notice us when in public, while they tell their friends in person or on the phone their deepest secrets. Also, as a group, we have over 500 years of experience and knowledge to draw from. We are retirees from the major industries of manufacturing, sales, banking, farming and administration. We even have a retired sheriff."

"You guys gather up all the town's gossip and secrets, then meet up and analyze all that information?"

"Precisely. After that unfortunate incident you were involved with, we realized we probably had the knowledge and skills to have helped you catch the murderer before you killed him in your living room."

"Now your group is working on the Vickers' murder?"

"We are. It is just beginning, but we have put together some initial hypotheses we are testing."

"That is something. I assume you are keeping your efforts as quiet as possible."

"Of course, otherwise we could not remain invisible. Nor can we have you getting clipped and leaving Kat without a dedicated can opener."

"I appreciate that. Kat does as well." I looked over to see her mostly stretched out on her pillow. A drop of drool was visible on the corner of her mouth. She knew how to put on a show.

"Seriously, though, the information we have been gathering does not look good. Last time, you had to deal with one person, Tammy's business partner. This time it looks like a whole conspiracy of people that are more dangerous than a lone real estate agent."

"I think I know what you are alluding to. It seems there might be several people involved with bringing marijuana into the county."

"Good, then you know to be careful. Meanwhile, we will keep doing our thing. I'll let you know what we come up with as soon as I can."

"Thanks Millard."

"Now I'm off to the joint next door. I have to torment Lottie."

"You two were made to torment each other. I guess it is just the old way of foreplay." Millard laughed so hard I thought I was going to have to defibrillate him. He was still chuckling when he went into Mable's.

I thought about what he had told me they were doing. I wasn't sure how well connected and organized they were, but it sounded like a good thing to me. I would take all the help I could get.

CHAPTER ELEVEN

My quiet day at the bookstore did not last. Bryan called me after lunch.

"James, I hate to bother you, but can you get away from the store this afternoon?"

"It is a slow day. What do you need?"

"We have information on a possible pot repacking location. We have our people ready to go, plus the state and DEA are sending agents. I'd like you to go with me. You'll stay in the car until the action is over, but then I'd like you to look the place over. See if you pick up anything we miss."

"Sounds like fun. Do I get to wear a bulletproof vest and

drink coffee with Woods and Sims, my two favorite state GBI agents?"

"That's a yes on the vest, and you can work on improving your workplace relationships any way you want. If that includes coffee-bonding, then go with it."

"Nah, that would just give them a reason to shoot me." Woods and Sims were the GBI agents from the year before that ended the investigation into Tammy Wilkins' death. Me catching the murderer they missed didn't put me on their Christmas card list.

"We leave in thirty minutes. Wear something dark and neutral. I'll have a vest for you in the car."

"I'll be ready by then." I pedaled to my house and changed clothes. Dark pants and a dark grey T-shirt. Not exactly stylish, but that was not the point. Kat came out of the crate as soon as we got back, and I let her stay inside with a snack. She was fine with that decision.

Bryan picked me up, and I rode with him. There were two deputy cars behind us, each staffed with two deputies. Bryan told me others would join us along the way.

From Warm Springs, we went south up Pine Mountain on the road toward Shiloh. Then we turned right to go along the top of the ridge, then left to descend the south side. Close to the bottom we turned again on a secondary road that had missed a few paving appointments. Then another turn onto a gravel road in name only. There may have been a few pieces of gravel on top of the dirt. The ruts were spine-jarring. Ahead were two other cars parked along the road, plus a black Hummer. One of the cars had two county deputies, while the other I recognized as a state-issue motor pool. My state-employee fan club was present. The Hummer was courtesy of the Drug Enforcement Agency, or DEA.

Everybody got out and had a quick conference. Bryan had told me everything was already planned out. This was a quick final check for everyone, in case anyone had any new information. Nobody did, so everyone got back into their vehicles. The DEA Hummer went first up a goat path that was more grass and ruts than a stable surface. It was speeding much too fast for these conditions.

"The DEA Hummer always goes first," Bryan said. "It has enough armor that it can handle most booby traps."

"Pot guys do booby traps? Why?"

"I don't know. But for some reason, they feel they have to. It's like they have a competition to see who is the most creative. The DEA learned the hard way they needed the armored version rather than the regular model."

"I suppose it is too late to let me out?"

"Yeah, sure is. Besides, you'd probably trip one of the mines or drop traps while walking out that we missed coming in."

"I want a raise in my consulting pay."

"You know what they say, naught times naught is still naught."

"Great, I'm in a booby trap-infested jungle learning redneck math from a police chief. And getting paid squat."

"Life is a wonder, isn't it? But you at least get to borrow a vest."

"What if they shoot at my head?"

"You'd best duck."

"I don't think the vest will do much for booby traps either. Does this come in a pants version?"

Bryan just gave me the look I'm sure he gave most consultants that asked a dumb question. The Hummer ahead took a hard left into a clearing with knee-high weeds. Bryan spun his wheels hard right and kept moving to give the cars behind us room to enter the clearing. In a few seconds, the vehicles formed a semicircle in the weeds. A large ravine was on the other side of the small clearing. The deep ditch ran up the wooded hillside at a slight angle, so I could not see what might be in it.

Bryan brought the car to an abrupt halt. "You stay put. There is a buried storage container a few feet into the ravine. We don't think anyone is here, but can't take any chances." He jumped out without waiting for a reply. I sat and watched as others exited vehicles. They pointed their weapons toward the ravine while using the cars to shield themselves. Two deputies ran along the edge of the clearing and toward the ravine with weapons out. They stopped and two more ran past them and stopped. Then the first two ran again and into the ravine. Everyone else waited beside their vehicles. I heard distant yells of "clear" and I saw everyone relax. Then they began walking toward the ravine. I stayed in the car after deciding I needed specific instructions to get out. Until I got a pair of pants to match my bulletproof vest, I would stay where I was and guard my important parts.

A few minutes later, Bryan came back to the car. "Are you ready to see how the drug kingpins run their empire?" he asked.

"I am," I said. I got out and followed him across the clearing and into the big ditch. Off to the left was a large square dark opening. A shipping container had been partially buried in the ravine to one side. Inside, it was dark and smelly. One deputy was still inside with a flashlight and all I saw was a dirty mattress on the floor and illiterate graffiti painted on the walls. A classy operation.

"Bryan, this is impressive in a dreary, destitute way."

"It is, isn't it? The drug guys live the high life."

"I'm not sure I can help with this. I see nothing that applies to the Vickers' investigation."

"No, I don't think so either. If this was a pot operation, they've been gone for months. But if nothing else, you got to see the kinds of places the pot folks are using in the county. Let's go."

On the way back, I asked Bryan something that was bothering me. "The container is out in the county. Why didn't the sheriff, General Custer, come out for the bust, since it was his jurisdiction?"

"He was informed, but declined. Said it was not worth his time, but sent two deputies to represent his department."

"Like he already knew there was nothing at that location."

"Exactly like that."

"I noticed his deputies were not much engaged. They didn't even have their weapons out when everyone else did. They also were not paying attention to where they walked, as if not concerned about traps."

"I noticed that too. Just going through the motions."

"Years ago, when large amounts of pot started coming into the country, I was in high school when a sheriff in north Georgia was arrested for running a pot operation up in the mountains. He provided protection, even distribution, for the pot coming in by the planeload. Some other county officials were involved as well. The money was too good for them to resist. Turns out about a dozen sheriffs around the state ended up getting caught for the same thing in just a few years."

"I've heard about it. Why did you know about it?"

"The sheriff in the mountains was known by my family. Otherwise, I would not have paid attention."

"Are you insinuating something about our Hamilton County chief law officer?"

"I don't know, but maybe. Could be that old ideas are being recycled."

"I don't know either. But I'll be watching and listening a little closer to the county drug affairs. There has been more pot in the county on his watch than before he was elected."

"Also, the shipping container we just saw. They use something that size for repacking pot? Do they live there and run a generator for electricity? I guess there is no running water. It seems awfully primitive."

"This could have been one of their facilities. They buy those containers for a couple thousand dollars, stick it somewhere in the country, and like you asked, run generators. No bathrooms, so hygiene is limited. They don't live there but might stay two days and nights solid to get a batch packed out. The containers are cheap enough there a probably dozen around the area at any given time. They can afford to rotate as needed to keep traffic down, then abandon them. Obviously, the one we just saw was abandoned and had been for some time. Local teenagers are probably using it for parties and such."

"Not the glamorous life I expected to see."

"Like everything, the bosses have nice houses and don't get their hands dirty while the workers endure the bad conditions and make a lot less."

"I don't see how you catch them, since they have a small footprint and small crews."

"We usually don't. Unless we have reliable information, it is almost impossible to find them."

"You are relying on tips and informants from local people."

"And sometimes tips from elsewhere, especially if they have competitors."

"How many groups are operating around here?"

"We have credible information that there are three in the area. Not sure if they are all in the county or not."

"That is more than I would have guessed."

"It is a good location to repack and distribute from. But yeah, it seems a little crowded. I'm surprised they aren't cannibalizing each other yet."

"Maybe it has begun if Vickers was involved in flying pot deliveries."

"We've been using that as our working hypothesis. Others might have wanted him gone, but we think his involvement in the pot business is what got him killed."

"Bryan, why did you ask me to go with you? I suspect you knew there was not going to be anything to see."

"You're right. Your presence was more to show my other law enforcement colleagues you are working on this case."

"Showing them you have some kind of hotshot consultant on staff."

"Not at all. Showing them you are under my protection."

"Uh, that means you suspect a colleague of wishing me harm. Why would they care? Unless they are in the business…"

"No reason for you to finish the sentence or for me to elaborate further. But I don't like where this case is going. Like we talked about earlier."

"OK, I understand. I'll need to be careful when working on certain leads."

"Yes, and if you get pointed to law enforcement individuals, you must come to me."

"I will since I don't want to get into a bad situation."

"That is wise. You can't always count on luck."

Driving up to Peachtree City to look at Mike Vickers' house was not as unpleasant as most Atlanta trips. It was on my side of Atlanta and there were back roads as well as the Interstate to get there. I had not been in a few years. I remembered it being a quiet place with lots of pine trees and golf carts. The carts were allowed on the streets, so many people used them to get around within the neighborhoods. Oddly enough, there were no golf courses there, just a few lakes. It was mostly residential but had enough retail areas and schools, so residents didn't have to leave other than commuting to work.

The community had some sections of larger expensive homes mixed with more moderate houses. Whatever the size or age of the house, it was more expensive than comparable homes outside Peachtree City. Location mattered, and prices went up inside the city limits. But there were some more affordable sections with smaller and older houses. I expected that was where I was going, following the address I had gotten from Bryan. Surprisingly, I found myself parked in front of a large brick home on one of the nicer streets instead. I sat in the car with the windows down to breathe in the atmosphere.

Police had already been on location as Bryan had told me the house had been searched, but nothing useful was found. I didn't need to go inside, anyway. I wasn't sure exactly why I was here, but I felt I needed to see it for myself. I knew so little about Mike Vickers that any details might help. But this address did not seem like a place owned by a single guy with a spotty work history. The big pines and smaller, planted hardwoods were encircled with azaleas and other ornamental bushes. Stacked stone beds with annuals were up closer to the house. I heard the sounds of children playing and occasionally a golf cart passed by. Lawnmowers buzzing in the distance. Two ladies in jogging outfits breezed past. I was getting a Stepford Wives vibe, and I could not see Mike Vickers living here.

There had to be something more I was missing. Or maybe less. What exactly was I looking at, a façade Vickers was putting out to the world? An investment to park money he supposedly didn't have? Everything about this location screamed modestly wealthy family, not pot smuggler. I was having a hard time reconciling this place with my interpretation of who Vickers was.

I looked at the house again. The yard was very nice. Too nice considering Vickers had not been here to cut grass, rake pine straw, or weed the beds. Vickers must have a lawn service handling the property.

I had not found anything of value here, just more frustration at seeing something I wasn't expecting. Cranking the car, I drove off to head back to Warm Springs. Two blocks down, I passed by a truck and trailer loaded with landscape equipment. An older man and two young men had just loaded up and were about to move to the next job. They looked hot and tired already. This neighborhood must keep them busy. Then it hit me. Who better to ask about Vickers than the people who were at his house once or twice a week for a few hours?

I turned around and pulled up next to the truck. "Hello, I am looking for a lawn service. I'm buying a house down the street and trying to find the service that keeps the yard. The realtor didn't know who had the contract."

"What is the address?" asked the older man. "It could be one of ours."

"It is 412 Oak Circle. Brick house about two blocks that direction on the left."

"Not one of ours. But if you need service, we can do it."

"Thanks, but I wanted to give the crew that has it the first shot at keeping it. But if you have a card or a contact, you will be next on the list." I thought that even though I was lying, maybe they would respect that I was being loyal to the original crew. Which could get me points if I considered switching to them.

The man rummaged through papers on the truck dash

and came up with a card. He handed to the younger man sitting by the window and he handed it to me.

"Thanks again. Do you happen to know who has that house?"

The three men had a conversation in Spanish. I never learned the language, so I had no idea what they were saying. Ten seconds later, they finished.

"I think I know," the man said to me. "Probably Fernando. I will call him and ask."

"I appreciate it."

The older man called and spoke to someone, again in Spanish. "It is his house, and he would like to keep it," he told me.

"Is that him you are speaking to?"

"Yes."

"Ask him if he could meet me there if he's not busy, so we can talk about it."

More conversation. "He says he can be there in thirty minutes."

"That is great. I'll be waiting."

The phone call ended, and the truck and trailer drove away. I drove out of the neighborhood to get a drink and then went back to wait in front of the house. A few minutes later, a landscape truck pulled up and the man I assumed was Fernando got out.

"Hello, are you Fernando?"

"Yes, and I have been working on the yard this year. You are buying it?"

"I'm in the process of getting it."

"I didn't know it was for sale. What happened to the owner?"

"He had to go away and won't be back. I'm looking at it before it is listed."

"You are looking to continue yard service?"

"Yes, and since you already know it I wanted to talk to you first."

"Thank you. I was charging the owner four hundred a month for the April to October season. November to March is optional, but if you need something like leaves raked or gutters cleaned, we do that on a per job basis."

"That sounds reasonable. Do you take checks?"

"We can, but prefer not to. Cash is better, and green is best, if you know what I mean."

"I can do cash. What kind of green are you saying?"

"If you are getting this place so quick, you must know Mike. If he is gone, then he must be in trouble. Anyway, he sometimes paid in green. Like in leaf."

"Oh, OK. I can do that as well."

"Very good. When do you want us to start?"

"As soon as I get the house. Meanwhile, are you caught up with Mike?"

"He is paid up through next week."

"I won't have the house by then, but I don't want to miss service. Can I give you a hundred to take it through the week after next?"

"Yes, that works."

I handed him a hundred-dollar bill. "I can get the other by the time the next payment is due."

"Mike is never coming back is he? A lot of police were here not long ago. But you don't look like a cop."

"That's right, Mike is gone. He seemed like a decent

guy, but he got crossways with somebody. And no, I'm definitely not with the police."

He seemed to relax a little after I declared I wasn't with the police. "That is a shame about Mike. He always treated me and my guys good. He gave us a little green to smoke, and it made the time go by faster. I'll miss that."

"Was it the Atlanta police or the county guys that showed up, or do you know?"

"The locals. About three cars that one day. A different car before that."

"A different police car was here before the big crowd?"

"Yeah, it was odd. Not local, it was a blue color. Had something like Hamilton on it. Nothing like that around here."

"Hamilton. Like Hamilton County Sheriff?"

"Could have been."

"Did it look like this?" I took out my phone and showed him a picture of General Custer's car, or at least one from his department. It was on their website. A distinctive light blue, with gold and black emblems and lettering.

"That's it."

"Do you remember when it was here?"

"It was out front two times I came by. One time, about two or three days before all the other cars were here. First time was about a week before that. Is that who got him?"

"I think so. The sheriff down there is, well…"

"I know the kind. Pull you over and lock you up because of how you look. Don't care about the law much."

"That's him."

"Mike never did anything to anybody. Smoked his weed and never caused problems. Doesn't seem right."

"No it doesn't. But I guess Mike was flying a plane full of something the sheriff objected to."

"Yeah, that can happen. But I wish it was not Mike."

"Fernando, do you know anything else about Mike's business? I'm asking because I'd like to make the sheriff's life more difficult."

"I don't think so. Mike loved to fly planes. He learned in the military and liked being back working with his buddies. He liked his weed and liked his yard. That's about it."

"He was working with his buddies?"

"Sounded like it. Friends he knew from overseas. I never saw or met them."

"Thanks Fernando for the talk."

"You aren't buying this house, are you?"

"No, I'm not. I'm looking for who got rid of Mike."

"I hope you find them. Since you don't need service, you want your money back?"

"No, keep it. Buy something to drink or smoke one and say something nice about Mike."

"I will."

"Have you seen his car around lately?"

"The new red one? No, not since that first police car came."

"Thanks, I appreciate your time. Make sure the realtor has your card. The house will be on the market once it clears the court. You know if you see the sheriff's car to stay away and not talk to them."

On the way home, I digested what I had learned. Vickers had come into money, probably illegally. Other than the flashy car, he put it into a safe but bland investment. A suburban house in a nice area. He took pride in his yard and smoked pot with his yard crew. He didn't seem like a drug kingpin.

Fernando mentioned Vickers was working with his buddies and implied they were also ex-military. I needed to talk to them to get more information on the why and who of Vickers' murder. In this case, my needs were at cross purposes with Bryan's. He was solving a murder and trying to shut down pot operations in his area. I just needed enough information about the victim to lead me to suspects. I did not much care about the pot operations in the county. Maybe I was ignorant about what they did and should try to stop it. After all, it was likely one or more of them killed Mike Vickers.

I found the revelation that a Hamilton County sheriff's car had been at Vickers' house more than once, both interesting and disturbing. Was it there for threats and intimidation leading to murder? Or was it a work delivery or pickup, or even a job offer? Why was it an official and distinctive car, and not a personal one or unmarked? Something else I needed to look into, but quietly.

It was too late to stop at the Georgia Archives. My research into the Roosevelt Institute and the people on and around the campus would have to wait. I would come back on a morning and spend the day.

I was stumped while making an important decision. Not about saving the world or working on the murder investigation, but on what to have for our picnic. Maybe not a pivotal component of our second date, but I did have standards when it came to food. Plus, I was trying to impress a date.

My thoughts on the menu were full of conflicting goals. Normally I went for items that would be safe, easy to carry and eat, and decent quality. I could compromise on most things related to food, but I never compromised on food safety. I roughed out a menu, made several sets of tweaks, then started over. Possibly I was overthinking the food.

The next list had some old favorites modified for the occasion.

Sandwiches would be bacon caprese. I liked caprese salad but thought a sandwich presentation would be nice and adding the bacon crossed it with a bacon-lettuce-tomato sandwich. A little messy for a picnic, but it would be worth it. Thinly sliced potatoes sprinkled with dill, roasted to crispy in the oven was the side dish. Dessert was a strawberry and champagne sorbet. Iced tea to drink of course. The packaging and presentation were key to the whole endeavor. But once organized, it was easy. It was good we were driving to a site and not hiking, as the back of my car held the equivalent of two picnic baskets.

I picked Donna up at her house and we were in Pine Mountain in less than fifteen minutes. Once in Pine Gardens, it took nearly as long to wind through the acres to a nice spot with a table in the woods near the lake chapel. The azaleas were in full bloom, so it made for a pleasant setting under the trees.

"James, this is a beautiful spot."

"I know, that is why I reserved it for us."

"You can't reserve spots in Pine Gardens."

"You caught me. But we are here during the week so not many people are around."

"What if somebody was already here?"

"There are probably eight or ten other spots nearly as nice as this one. We would have found a nice place no matter what."

"What's on the menu for today?"

"A simple meal. Sandwiches, chips, and dessert."

Donna glanced at my backseat. "You say simple, but all that stuff back there says something else."

"There may be some assembly required."

"That will be some instruction manual. Two coolers, two boxes, and two thermoses."

"It appears a lot, but it really isn't. Shall we dine?"

"Let's dine. I'll take the boxes."

I took the coolers and one thermos to the table, following Donna. Then I unpacked everything from the coolers in order, which took up half the table.

"OK, Donna now for the first box. Here we have toasted bread and fresh made potato chips, both still warm."

"They might be warm, but they will be soggy."

"Nope, I use modern science to defeat sog."

Donna opened the box and started laughing. "James, I've not seen this combination before, whether for food or anything else. Not sure whether you are smart or insane."

"The proof is whether the bread and potatoes are still warm and crisp."

Donna removed the two packages wrapped in tin foil poked with small holes. Then she took out the hand warmers usually found in the pockets of hunters in the winter. Next she pulled out a plastic canister, full of the white stuff usually found in damp basements to get rid of moisture. She peeled back the corner of each tin foil package and tore off a small piece of toast and a potato chip. Both were still warm and crispy.

"Genius it is."

"Oh, was there a doubt?"

"What are we putting on the bread?"

"I have sliced fresh tomato and mozzarella slices in

these containers, fresh basil leaves in this one, and bacon in the other. Now here is the one necessity to begin your sandwich."

"Which is?"

"Avocado paste. Better than mayonnaise and keeps the liquids from making the toasted bread gooey."

"Show me."

I built a sandwich and handed it to her. She bit into it. "Oh, James, you can make me these on our honeymoon." I nearly dropped the knife I was using to build the other sandwich. I thought she was going to choke between laughing and devouring the sandwich. She didn't, so I carried on and poured her an iced tea and handed her a plate with chips.

"You looked a little distressed a moment ago. Was it something I said?"

"Possibly. I believe you called me a genius."

"Psssh, that wasn't it. I believe it was the implication of our upcoming nuptials."

"You've only had two of my meals. Aren't you jumping the gun a little?"

"Oh no, I expect many more of these. I'm sure you have quite a catalog. And you underestimate how much I treasure good food I don't have to make."

"I'll have to put in some language to that regard in the prenuptial agreement."

"Oh, already thinking of contingencies."

"I have to protect myself. Some taco truck may come along and woo you away from me." We both laughed.

"Don't worry, James, I'm not in the market for another husband. How about you?"

"I'm absolutely certain I don't want a husband."

"You know what I mean. This may be too soon to even be talking about it, but we are grown adults. Very grown based on age, so we might as well be frank."

"True. I guess I am not in the market for a wife. Someday, maybe, but it is not something I even think about. Most days, it's about getting through life and enjoying what I have. If someone comes along and makes it better, then I'm all for it. What about you?"

"About the same as you. It would be nice to have someone, but then I remember how the not-quite-right someone in my house every day and night is not great. And all that negative effort to get clear of it. I would rather enjoy my days, like you, and find someone that fits into that life."

"I agree. I don't think a civil or religious ceremony is necessary between two people that have a working relationship. Although it is an unfortunate reality in our society that legally it is sometimes necessary to protect someone in case of a medical issue or death. Someone I know had a long-term relationship late in life. Then he died and his partner got kicked out of the house by the adult children and had to start over."

"That's awful. But marriage is not the best answer."

"No, it is not. Some countries in Europe have a registered partnership agreement for those kinds of things. Two people live together and their rights are protected, especially if they have kids together. But no messy divorce. If they no longer get along, one or both move out with predetermined assets going along."

"That seems like a better system."

"In many cases, it is. Are we done with this conversation now?"

"That is a bit abrupt, but I think so. Why?"

"We have sorbet for dessert. Also pie from Mable's if you don't like sorbet. But mostly because I need to tell you something."

"First of all, I love sorbet. The wedding is back on. But wait, tell me what you need to say. If it's bad, I might have to go find the taco truck."

I dug the sorbet out of a thermos and placed it in two bowls. Donna sniffed it and broke into a grin. "No pie is necessary. This smells wonderful. Now tell me you darkest secret."

"You've heard about the recent murder where the body was found near the road on Pine Mountain?"

"Of course. The one where you are working with Bryan and the police to find the killer."

"That is what I wanted to tell you. But you already knew."

"It's a small town. Now, for the next two minutes, I require quiet. I'm meditating with this sorbet. I hope to become one with it." I gave her the requested quiet time. It was nice to be with someone that enjoyed food so much. Of the million things two people look for in each other, this was a promising development.

"OK, I've decided to forego the taco truck forever," she said. "Why did you want to tell me you were working on the investigation?"

"I wasn't sure if you knew. I didn't mention it last time since I was just starting and I didn't know much, nor if I would continue. But I didn't want to scare you off if you were uncomfortable with it."

"I'm an author. I am comfortable with almost anything. I research and make up all kinds of things for my books. I rarely have murders in my romance genre, but it does not bother me that you are involved in the investigation. But thanks for telling me."

"No problem. You know, the chapel is right over there. We can go ahead and make this official."

"Nice try. But I'm not committing until you make me a chocolate cake. If it's better than my grandma's, then maybe you have a shot."

"A high target, but now I know the game. Want to walk around and see the butterfly house?"

"Absolutely. We also need to talk about our golf outing."

For the next two hours, we walked around looking at some of the thousands of native azaleas in bloom. Pine Gardens was known for those this time of year. The dogwoods were nice, too. We made it around to a planted area full of tulips. But we were at least a week too late, as many of the blooms were gone. The field was an expanse of green and brown instead of the palate of bright colors I once knew in the Netherlands. I didn't mind since the company and weather were nice.

I drove us to another section of the Gardens. We parked near a nondescript two-story building with glass visible up high. Inside there was a lobby, with a glass door going into a vestibule with a high-speed fan blowing from above. Then another glass door led us into an indoor hot house full of tropical plants. But the genuine attraction was the multitude of brightly colored tropical butterflies throughout the space. Just about every color was represented in the wings fluttering around us. There was an undercurrent of over-ripe fruit throughout, because cut tropical fruits were placed to feed the butterflies needing that instead of plant nectar. We spent half an hour inside trying to see every version of the winged beauties, but then it was time to leave.

"That was nice," Donna said. "I have not been here in years."

"I don't go often but today it seemed like a good idea."

"It was."

"Know what else is a good idea?"

"What?"

"I've got my golf clubs in back. Want to go to the driving range?"

"You bet I do."

At the driving range I watched Donna hitting golf balls. She was definitely better than me, but I didn't care. I got to see her athleticism, just making her more attractive. After nearly an hour, I took Donna home. She kissed me before getting out. I thought it was another successful date. Once again, I had not said or done anything to send her running off.

CHAPTER FOURTEEN

I had a hunch about the investigation and called my relatives, or rather Emma's family, and asked them over for lunch. I traded lunch invites every three or four months with Sam and Irene. She liked to come over to campus to walk and get her steps in. She had not been on campus other than driving through it before I invited them for the first time. We walked the loop and quad that day, and she loved it. Sometimes she and a friend came over to walk during the day. It was a safe and easy place to walk.

I cut up a chicken and put it on the grill. It had marinated overnight, and I applied a dry rub before grilling. Now I added some vinegar-based sauce every fifteen minutes. No reason to eat chicken if it wasn't flavorful. I thick-sliced some fresh tomatoes, then added a shaved-thin slice of a large Vidalia onion on top. Spices, lemon juice, and a mozzarella-parmesan blend were sprinkled on each slice before adding them to the grill. They only needed a few minutes, then I removed them along with the chicken. A batch of sautéed new potatoes and a salad finished the meal. I checked the cooked chicken on the counter a last time with my fast-read thermometer and determined it was done. I considered it poor taste to send my guests home after inoculating them with Salmonella.

My only dessert was never simpler—fresh watermelon slices. I had found one at the farmer's market that appeared ripe. It was too early for local ones, unfortunately. I put the slices into the freezer for a few minutes to give a slight crust freeze. Crunchy watermelon was always fun.

Sam and Irene arrived, and we ate and traded some local gossip about campus and the Cove, where they lived. After the watermelon, Irene wanted to go walk. Sam and I went to the porch as I had told him I wanted to talk about some recent events. Irene smiled knowingly and left to circle the campus.

"James, seems you are curious about something. Anything to do with the body found up on the hill?"

"Maybe, but indirectly. The police seem to think he might have been into pot smuggling. I'm not suggesting you are, but I believe you might know people that might have some connections to that."

"Could be. What are you thinking about, or needing to ask?"

"I'm not exactly sure. But something I wonder about is

why do something like that around here? It seems too far out of the way of the markets."

"There is a lot of activity for such a rural area. But you know we are close to lots of larger towns and the Interstates. It is easy to do business in a place like this where you know everyone. If the police are looking into you, that gets around very fast in these parts. Much like the old bootleg days. If the federal agent was coming to look for your moonshine still, you normally had two days' advance notice. The revenue man had to stay somewhere, buy gas for his car, eat at a restaurant, that kind of thing. Minutes later, the word was out that a federal revenue agent was in town. Everybody knew he was hunting for stills."

"I understand all of that. My grandfather ran a moonshine still and business in north Georgia. But wouldn't it be hard to hide a large marijuana distribution operation because this place is so small?"

"Not at all. You know those large shipping containers? I think they are around forty feet long and ten feet wide. That is about the space they need. Or half a basement."

"I had a look at one recently. Bryan took me for a ride along to an abandoned one. Before that, I imagined a big warehouse with loading docks."

"No need for all that stuff. All they do is open the bales, reweigh across scales into smaller amounts that are sealed in bags. A week's worth of repackaged pot could fit into a van or two."

"I know those containers are used all over the county. Farmers are using them for storage. Even the deer camps have them to lock up their equipment."

"All true. Some of those containers are buried. The end-of-the-world preppers use them as bunkers."

"A pot operation really can hide easily. I guess I was thinking about the large growing operations, where they grow it indoors."

"There is one of those around here too. Those require much better security and ways to hide what they do. Their high consumption of electricity at night is how a lot of them used to get caught. They need a lot of juice for grow lights and ventilation. Smart police would look at energy usage in rural areas like that to find likely grow houses."

"How do they get around that now?"

"A lot of them use generators for electricity. Some are even using solar power. Less of that, as the DEA helicopters look for large arrays of solar panels as a red flag for growers."

"I remember how some used to grow it outside."

"A few still do because here you have a lot of vacant cutover timberland, national forests and a huge state park. It is risky, but some of the locals plant small plots around the county. They mostly do it for themselves and local sales, as they can't compete with the importers on quality or quantity."

"From what you said, neither the DEA nor the police have any real chance of locating one of the import operations."

"Not without specific knowledge of where it is."

"You mentioned a local indoor grower. Are they likely to be involved in the recent violence? Maybe they are looking to reduce competition."

"It is possible. I can find out more, but I'll need a few days."

"I don't want you to get in trouble for my sake. Don't do it if there is a chance it will come back to bite you."

"I won't. I know all the locals. Are you going to share the information with the police or DEA?"

"No, what I'm looking for is general information to figure who is killing and why. But eventually, that person needs to go down, whether by police or other means."

"That eases my mind. I'm sure the other interested parties want the violence to stop as well. Either for the obvious need to protect themselves, but also protect their business from the scrutiny a murder brings."

"On that subject, something is bothering me. It does not make sense to kill someone, even a rival, over importing pot once a week. Especially the brutal way it was done."

"It sent a message, maybe. But way out of proportion."

"Yeah it was. Have you heard any rumors about anything else going on?"

"Not really. Pot interests have been in this county for a long time."

"Do you think one of the operations is getting into hard drugs or something worse?"

"I have not heard anything. And if the groups are who I think they are, hard drugs don't make sense. And there has been no mention of them aligning with a Mexican cartel or one of the South American organizations, if that is what you are thinking."

"That was my next question. I guess the last question is whether this might have been personal."

"I don't see it. I barely knew him, but Vickers was a

quiet guy, didn't offend anyone. He had the military background but didn't bully anyone. I'm not aware of anyone that had a problem with him. Certainly no enemies that would have done those kinds of things to him."

"I appreciate the talk. Let me know if you hear anything else. And please be careful if you ask around. Whoever did that to Vickers is still here, and probably looking to cover his tracks."

"I've got it. I didn't stay alive and out of jail this long without being smart. And knowing what not to know. Just kidding about the jail part. Irene keeps me out of trouble."

"Sure she does."

"She does try, and we have not been around that lifestyle for a long time. It is kind of hard to describe what it is like trying to get away from something like that and being a better person."

"I know exactly what that is like."

"Come on, I doubt it. You don't look or act like a bank robber or smuggler."

"I'm not. But some in my family were. I made the decision to get away and stay away."

"I guess you do know what it is like, then."

"Very much."

"How long have you been out?"

"I left when I was eighteen. I was around enough to know what was going on. It had a certain appeal, but I somehow had enough sense to know how it would end. Eventually, I'd have been dead or in jail for decades."

"Those must have been some serious people."

"They were. I see Irene coming back. Time to change the conversation."

"Good idea. Should I tell Irene anything about this last part of our conversation?"

"It is OK with me. No harm in her knowing, unless she held my outlaw family against me."

"She wouldn't. Besides, you'd be right at home in the Cove. Not all the stories we tell about the place are past tense."

"What stories?" Irene asked. She heard the very last part of Sam's comment as she came on the porch.

"Cove stories, the ones about people misbehaving and getting in trouble."

"Oh yes, there are plenty of those. Lately the chop shop down the road has been busy. Stolen cars are a thing right now since prices are up for used cars and parts."

"Speaking of that, Vickers' car has not been found yet," I said. "I wonder if it was taken by his killers or if it got stolen later."

"What was it?"

"Bright red Mustang, some kind of special edition. I heard it had racing harnesses instead of seat belts."

"New?"

"I think less than a year old."

Sam and Irene traded a look. "A car like that is real popular. Maybe enough to get laundered and passed on, rather than chopped into parts."

"Laundered?"

"It's a tedious process of removing the Vehicle Identification Number from the car. Each window is etched, and it is cast in the metal of a number of major parts of the car. Takes effort to get rid of all those. After that, it usually gets painted a different color. Even then, it is safer to send it to Mexico than keep it around."

"So it could still be in the area?"

"Maybe. But even if it is, the car will be gone somewhere soon. It could already be in fifty parts and distributed."

"I'll let Bryan know. He can track it down if it is still around."

"That is a good idea. Let law enforcement handle it. Some of the choppers don't take kindly to people poking around."

"Thinking about it, Mike's cousin runs a towing company."

"What's the name?"

"Doyle Vickers."

Sam and Irene traded another look. "James, let Bryan deal with it. Doyle is known for a short temper and lack of judgement."

"You know him?"

"No, but I know about him. He's always mad and always looking for an angle. If he tows your car, you'd better take everything of value out of it first."

"An opportunist then. Could he have been involved in the murder of a family member?"

"Depends on how much he had to gain. If it was a lot, and low risk, then yeah."

"I'll have to get to know him. Maybe get him to tow a car."

"Just be careful. If he thinks you are looking at him for murder, it could go sideways real quick."

CHAPTER FIFTEEN

"Hey Bryan, do you have a minute?" I was at the cafeteria for a quick breakfast and saw Bryan on the way home.

"I actually have five minutes for my ace consultant, especially if you are not asking for more money."

"No money needs today. But I would like to requisition one of those fancy bulletproof vests for Kat."

"Can't do. The only animal vests I can get are for dolphins."

"I know you are kidding, but that could be true, could it not?"

"I would not be surprised if it were true. What do you have?"

"I know Mike's car has not been found. I heard Doyle has access to a chop shop, so maybe that's an avenue to look at."

"Could be, and I recently heard something similar."

"Also, I heard from the landscape guys that work at Mike's house. They had two interesting bits of information. First, they thought he was working with his buddies from his military days. And they knew about his involvement with the pot business. He sometimes gave it to them."

"That is interesting. Given our proximity to Columbus and the military base, I bet they are down there. What's the other part?"

"Before Vickers was killed, a police car started showing up at his house. A particular car."

"What was it, or are you keeping me in suspense?"

"A Hamilton County Sheriff's car."

"Are you sure?"

"He described it to me, a sky-blue car with gold and black letters. I showed him a picture, which he confirmed."

"I believe him. That is a distinctive car. I don't think any other police forces have that color scheme."

"Do you think they were investigating Vickers or something more nefarious?"

"I don't know, but I would like to find out."

"That's all I had, for now."

"Thanks, I'll put that in the case file and figure out how to go about getting into the Sheriff's business."

"Good luck."

I got to the bookstore and opened up. Kat and I spent the morning doing bookstore things. Well, I did, while she mostly napped in the window. It was good for her vitamin D metabolism, so I didn't mind.

After lunch, Irene called and asked if they could stop by. I told her to meet me at the house and went home after closing the bookstore. One of the few perks of ownership was closing when I needed to. I wanted to hear what they had found out.

I welcomed them with ice tea on the front porch. We sat to talk.

"James, you may have guessed we aren't fully retired," Sam said. "We dabble in other things and almost all of those things are legal."

"We do a lot with edibles," Irene added. "No pot or other things because pot is still illegal in this state and at the federal level. We won't take the risk anymore, because we have too much to lose."

"From getting arrested, I suppose," I said.

"That, and because of what happened to Mike Vickers," Sam said. "Competition can be deadly."

"I get that. But aren't edibles illegal, at least some of them?"

"It is confusing," Sam continued. "There are many different versions of edibles. Laws across states and even the federal level are all over the place, and they change nearly every year. Even most police departments are not current on the latest statutes. Edibles get the benefit of the doubt, mostly because you never hear about violent criminals hopped up on edibles. Nor are there stories about vicious edible smugglers."

"That is true. I don't ever remember hearing those kinds of stories."

"Edibles are for people looking for something mellow," Irene said. "A lot of the market is for older people that need something for chronic pain."

"That keeps law enforcement from taking a hard stance I imagine."

"It does," Sam said. "Have you noticed the video poker machines in the convenience stores around here?"

"I have, and the closest gas station has a couple."

"Those can be legal or illegal, depending on current law and how winnings are paid out," Sam said. "But they are sitting there in a retail store in broad daylight."

"Those, just like edibles, are a grey area," Irene said. "No obvious public harm, so no harsh enforcement."

"Exactly," Sam continued. "That is where we conduct business. Margins aren't big, but the risk is small."

"How does your business work, in general?" I asked.

"We buy wherever we find the best products at the lowest prices. We resell at a markup mostly to businesses. Buying and selling it in states where it is legal, or at least not specifically illegal. We pay our taxes and don't do anything dumb."

"That model keeps you out of trouble."

"Well, our risk is due to state laws," Sam said. "To get the best stuff, we travel out of state. Transporting across state lines for those states with strict laws could be a problem."

"But not if you don't get caught," Irene said. "Imagine a normal couple going on vacation in a camper, going the speed limit, and not partaking of their transported product. It is very low risk."

"That's an accurate description of what we do," Sam

added. "We can go up to Maine and out to Colorado once a year, or wherever we need to. So far, it has not been a problem."

"I guess that is why you know something about the current state of pot affairs in the county."

"Yes, plus some past activities we don't talk about anymore."

"How much more do you know about the current situation?"

"I don't think we can add much more to what you've already found or guessed. Mike Vickers was the pilot for a pot smuggling operation. He was flying it into Hamilton County. Once here it was weighed, repacked and distributed in the southeast. It was a new group, but they were competing against an established operation. Also, a newer, fairly small grower is in the area. That was the one I mentioned."

"Basically, it is what I already had heard or guessed regarding Mike. The people that Mike Vickers was working with, though, any chance I could get into contact with them? Unofficially, of course. I'd like to find out what they know about his death. I don't need to know about their business."

"Maybe. It is one of those 'I know a guy that knows a guy' kind of daisy chain."

"Somebody I met at Mike Vickers' house mentioned he was in business with his military buddies. Is that a good or bad thing if I want to talk to them? I don't have any military background, and will they be paranoid talking to an outsider?"

"Should not be a problem. I doubt you will know their names, anyway. But they will want to stay anonymous."

"True, and I don't need to know them. Maybe we should meet, so I don't see their faces either."

"Even better. How do you plan to do that?"

"I don't know, maybe we all wear balaclavas on our faces, or talk through the wall of a transport container."

"I've heard worse ideas. Better than meeting in a dark parking garage."

"Especially since there are none of those within an hour's drive."

"I'll check on my end. I'd say it is no better than a fifty percent chance they will want to talk to you."

"That's fifty percent more of a chance than I have right now. Any idea who is running the established operation? I've heard it might be a problem."

"This is where it gets tricky for you. Rumor has it for quite a while the Sheriff is in charge of the other operation. Whether it is all his, or he runs it for someone else, is up for debate."

"Yeah, that is a problem. Sheriffs have a lot of sway in the county."

"They do, and that is just on the legal side of what they control. A sheriff has even more pull on the illegal side of things. You don't want to get involved or go asking around about his business. There is no way that he won't hear about it. Then a traffic stop goes bad when they plant a kilo of pot in the trunk and you get shot resisting arrest."

"That would be bad for my health. I'll let Bryan handle that side of the inquiry. But there is something I should be able to check into without alerting him."

"What's that?"

"If the Sheriff is taking in significant amounts of cash, maybe a million or more per week, it has to go somewhere. I can follow the money with no one knowing. He must have a business somewhere he launders the money, or he goes to the Caribbean regularly to make deposits in his offshore accounts."

"Yeah, that should be safe. Just don't ask those questions in the county. Or anywhere within an hour's drive."

"I won't. You also said there was a grower in the area."

"Supposed to be somebody growing some high-end boutique pot. Mainly for wealthy customers in Atlanta and Florida, although I think it goes anywhere there are customers willing to shell out lots of money for regular pot with a cute name."

"I have not heard about boutique pot before."

"Supposed to be the best hybrid genetics, grown in specific conditions. Special dirt, music, and, of course, it is organic. I think it is more about marketing than anything real."

"Maybe some soil amendments and genetic improvements could make a slight difference, but yeah, the rest is embellished marketing. Must be trying to create a name brand market. Is the grower likely to be dangerous enough to commit murder?"

"I doubt it. No reason for a new pot smuggling operation in the area to cause any issues with the grower. It is highly unlikely there is any competition for the targeted customer base."

"It is something I need to check into just the same."

"I have a good idea who it is. I heard about a guy in the

south part of the county that was trying to convert his special pot into high-end edibles. But it was also smoke and mirrors, just more marketing. If it is him, I'll let you know when I confirm."

"Thanks."

"Anyway, I'll have that information soon, plus the potential meeting with Vickers' partners if they are agreeable."

"I do appreciate it, and my thanks to both of you."

CHAPTER SIXTEEN

Later in the afternoon, I had to get to Pine Mountain for a semi-date. I was not sure what else to call a golf outing with someone who was going to destroy me while I had to be nice and funny. At least Donna would have fun. I had watched her hit golf balls after the picnic, and while I knew the range was much different from the golf course, she was an excellent golfer. She always hit the ball well and did not have hooks and slices. The biggest part of being successful at golf was consistently hitting it straight. Even knowing that she was that good, we had made plans to play today. Being out with her and admiring her athleticism was too good to pass up.

I would have picked her up on the way, but she was

driving as she had places to go afterward in Pine Mountain and Hamilton. I drove into the long and winding road past the Pine Gardens entrance through fields and woods to get to the course on the back side. I got my clubs out as Donna pulled up and parked. We went into the clubhouse and checked in. Then on to the course for the fun to begin.

It was a nice late afternoon, with springtime temperatures a little higher than usual. We nearly had the course to ourselves, so no pressure to keep moving since there was no one behind us. It was an easy and enjoyable way to spend time once I let go of caring how I played. Which was the attitude I needed to play slightly better.

Donna was like a machine hitting the ball. Her shots went straight and almost always where she aimed. She stayed on the fairways and was always on the green with the minimum number of shots necessary. Other than a couple of missed putts, she was a textbook golfer. Her natural talent and thousands of hours of practice really showed.

I, however, was another story. If she was a finely manicured estate, I was a junkyard. My accuracy was inconsistent, and although I could hit the ball a long way, it often went looking for difficult places to land. Woods, creeks, sand bunkers, and even the lake once. It was a version of adventure golf—where would the ball go next? Despite those frustrations, I had fun. Donna and I kept up a conversation, and she helped me celebrate the good shots. She wasn't too tough on me after the bad shots, nor did she bother telling me all the things I was doing wrong either. She was a true athlete in her natural element, but always a nice person.

When done after nine holes, she ended up two shots over par. I was nine over, and that was with the benefit of a few incredibly lucky shots. On a full course, she was close to a par golfer, and I'd be lucky to break a score of 90. Perhaps I should practice more. Alone, it was no fun, but maybe Donna would take pity on my game and go with me a few times a month. Back at the clubhouse we sat down a few minutes before she had to leave. We both got iced tea to drink.

"James, I can tell you used to play by the way you evaluate the upcoming shots and handle the course. Also, that it's been a while, because of your inconsistent contact. But oh my, you sure are lucky. Some of those tee shots, the chip-in shot, and the way you dropped the twenty-five-foot putt. Then the eighty yards on bare dirt under the trees onto the green, after swatting the ball with a one-iron. You must be a trick shooter."

"Yep, and most of those strokes would have been unnecessary if I had made better previous shots."

"Still, you would be dangerous with training and practice."

"I'll skip the training. But I'd like to keep playing. Maybe enough to start getting better."

"I'd be happy to play once a week if you can work it into your schedule."

"I think I can make that work. Actually, if you are serious, I'll definitely make it happen."

"Good. How is the investigation going?"

"OK I guess. It appears it might be moving toward people and activities slightly more dangerous than my last foray into a murder investigation."

"James, didn't you tell me you were seconds from being shot in the head the last time?"

"Uh, well, yeah, that was about to happen."

"Then this investigation must be a lot more dangerous. Are you being careful?"

"I think so, at least so far."

"That is not very reassuring. If you get yourself shot in the head who is going to play golf with me?"

"Donna, I think most of the men in the county would love to play golf with you."

"Aren't you sweet? But trying to change the subject is not going to work. Just tell me you will be careful."

"I will be. Believe me, I have no interest in being in a dangerous spot."

"You say that, but you seem to have a penchant for finding trouble."

"I guess so. Sort of like my golf game."

Donna left, and I went back home. She was right, of course. I did need to be more careful than usual. At home, I began my more careful life by working in the yard and rerouting drainage away from the cottage. Too much rainwater went downhill from the house, across the yard and toward the cottage. I preferred to keep the foundation dry as possible. After fixing all the termite damage, I had no interest in letting the new foundation rot.

I showered, and Kat and I had dinner. By the time I let Kat out, I heard an engine approach. I knew the sound well.

Standing on the porch, I surprisingly heard it accelerate, then saw Millard zip by. In front of my house, he spun the steering wheel and hit the gravel parking lot next door, which was the police station. Millard drifted the UTV into a graceful curve and ended up back on the road facing me, after doing a 180-degree turn. He sat there grinning, waiting for the inevitable reaction. The station door opened, and Bryan came out to see the commotion, then shook his head at seeing Millard.

Millard waved and slowly came over to my house. This must have been the behavior Lottie talked about. I thought she had been exaggerating. Despite his flamboyant driving, his vest was heather tweed.

"Let's go for a ride," he said.

"After that stunt I'm going to require a racing harness and more life insurance."

"I'll take it easy on you, old man." Strong words for someone more than twenty years older than me.

I took a chance and climbed in. Kat did not bother to wave goodbye when I waved at her. Millard drove us down to the lake, then around it. He parked under the trees not far from the stand of wax myrtles where I had first spotted what turned out to be Tammy Wilkins' body.

"This is where your career in crime solving began, isn't it? Millard asked.

"I have not thought of it like that, but I guess so."

"I wanted to give you the group analysis on this latest murder. We thought you might benefit from what we have so far. Bryan has a staff and a network to draw from, and the state GBI folks have an even larger network. That puts you at a disadvantage, so we intend to pick up the slack. That will make you more competitive."

"This not only keeps you guys active but also is tied into

your betting network on who finds the murderer and when?"

"Of course. A little extra emphasis to keep us from getting lazy."

"OK, what do you have?"

"Just general information, some things you might not have worked out yet or had time to discover. But important enough that you could use for your investigation. Ask questions as I go."

"Sure. But will I remember everything?"

"Not a chance. Your cognitive skills are likely already diminished. Here is your outline." Millard pulled out a leather case and fished out a sheet of paper with bullet points printed on it. Then he handed me a full binder with the details.

"I appreciate your thoroughness and thoughtfulness."

"First, we have an analysis of the marijuana market, both the legal and illegal trade. What that gives you is an estimate of what kind of money you are trailing. Might be easier to trace back to the bad guy or guys. Second, we did a logistical analysis on the practical aspects of the trade. Including how much marijuana weighs and how much cash weighs. For you, you can figure out what kind of transport and storage might be used to bring the pot in and the cash out. Last, we have some ideas on where the cash goes in regard to laundering it into legitimate enterprises, if it is actually happening. Gives you another trail to look for and trace back to the culprits."

"Millard, this is awfully professional."

"It should be since we were all professionals once. Use this to catch the criminals before your competition."

"I appreciate the help. Those betting on me must be getting worried."

"Not really, but we are evening the odds to hedge our bets. Now, do you know how much a bale of compressed marijuana weighs or how big it is when packaged for transport?"

"I have no idea."

"It varies, but one ton compressed into multiple bricks could fit into the cargo hold of a small plane. But many small planes could not carry that much on one trip, depending on distance flown and fuel weight. The tables we included show plane types with those variables in the binder. We also have included the volumes and capacities of cargo vans and various other common vehicles. We also calculated the same weights and volumes for cash, based on amounts and denominations."

"That will come in handy and give me some ideas on where to look."

"Our analysis on potential money laundering schemes may be less helpful. About all we could do was narrow down the possibilities available around here. But we included a section on likely places where illegal money could be stashed offshore with little scrutiny."

"Before I read it, do you think it more likely the pot crews are sending money out to hide it or keeping it close and laundering through legitimate businesses?"

"Based on the calculated incomes and local costs to the crew, we don't think the remaining money could be laundered locally. There is too much of it coming in regularly to hide. Atlanta is a potential place to launder it with a business, but not Hamilton County. Our best guess is the cash goes out."

"How much?"

"Rounding off the numbers, and making it easier to scale up or down, think about a ton of pot coming in per week. For a premium retail price of $1000 per pound, that grosses 2 million dollars a week. Half of that goes to buy it from the legal sources and pay the help. So, one ton nets about a million in cash a week."

"Thanks again, Millard. This will help quite a bit."

"That is what we want, James. Now let's get you home so you can start studying, then go catch the crooks."

At home, I began studying the binder Millard had given me. I skimmed through it first and was impressed with the data collection and analysis. These guys were legitimately putting out first class research. I had never thought about pot weight and volume before. Even more surreal was thinking about the weight and volume of money. Examples in the report showed a million dollars in bills as weighing 22 pounds and fitting into a backpack if it was all hundred-dollar bills. Weight went up to 45 pounds and a large duffel if in fifties; 110 pounds and two large duffels if in twenties.

What little I knew about the operation Mike Vickers was involved with made me think it was smaller than a ton of pot a week. But still, it was a nice chunk of profit even if he flew in half that much or less per week. A thousand pounds would be about right for a plane. Probably a little less based on the charts in the binder. I didn't know what plane Mike flew, but I needed to find out.

If the established operation was twice as big, that meant a large volume of cash was moved out of the county. If the money was in mixed denominations, then at least 75 pounds a week. It would fill a 55-gallon drum each month. So where was the money going?

The binder gave me several options if it was staying in the region and being laundered. Likely scenarios were: real estate, precious metals, gambling, and farm equipment. There was a detailed section for each, along with reasons for and against their use, both within the county and in the neighboring counties. Precious metals were ruled out because of regulations governing large-scale purchases. Real estate was more interesting because it was divided into sections for timber land, orchards, fish farms, and chicken farms. Again, with reasons mostly against why those would not be attractive places for laundering. It was noted that unusual activity was detected with the purchase of several farms at the same time; all were formerly chicken farms. That tracked with what Sam had told me about the new grower in the county.

Lastly, there was a short section on the places outside the country where large quantities of money could be sent. The usual places made the list, including the Cayman Islands and Switzerland. Two places not known to me were Belize and Panama. A special note was added that both Belize and the Caymans could be accessed by boat from the US.

I had not digested it all yet, but it was all useful information. Now I had to put it to good use and find Mike's killer. One thought haunted me; what if the killer was not involved in the pot business? Then all this was for nothing, and tomorrow I was putting myself at risk of a dead end. That was my chipper thought as I went to sleep.

CHAPTER SEVENTEEN

The next morning, I was on my way to doing something extremely foolish. And just after promising Donna that I would not put myself in a bad spot. Wearing my hiking clothes and boots, I was walking across a large clear-cut with freshly planted pines about knee-high. The trail I was on was one rut of an old logging road, although really more red clay mud. Somewhere at the end of this road, I would meet Mike Vickers' partner or partners. I hoped he was friendly because I was far from civilization or any authority that might protect me. Sam had made contact and set up a meeting.

Once Sam gave me the address and directions, I looked

up the place on a satellite map. A rectangular corner lot of about 150 acres with paved roads fronting two sides, and a dirt road on part of a third side. My directions were to go to an address, which was a metal gate on the highway, park, and walk up the dirt logging road. From the map, I knew this logging road intersected with another that turned hard right and went to the other highway. There was also an ATV trail off to the left that went to the dirt road. Someone chose well because they would have at least two escape routes.

The directions said to come alone, so I had. But I also had my phone on and dialed into Bryan's phone. He wasn't happy about me going alone, but I needed to get a story. I knew there was no chance they would talk to Bryan, as the risk of prison was too great. But out here alone, if something happened, it would be too late to save me, but at least he could arrest someone. That made me feel special.

I assumed the meeting would be somewhere around the intersection of the logging roads and ATV trail. I arrived and did not see anyone. But there was a hunting blind, one of those tents that set up quickly with camouflage print. I think they were mostly used for turkey hunting. I guess I knew what that made me. As I approached, I heard a voice call out.

"Stop there. Hold your arms straight out and slowly turn all the way around."

I did as instructed. I heard two voices talking low in the tent. "Now what?" I asked.

"Come on up to the tent. I needed to see you were not carrying a weapon."

I walked closer, imagining at least two people inside holding guns pointed at me. Even if I could get my small 9mm pistol out of my ankle holster before they shot me, I didn't know exactly where to shoot since I could not see into the tent. I would not even try unless I had no other choice. Their approach to the meeting was somewhat comical but effective. They could see me, but I could not see them while we talked. They would also see me coming and going for a long distance, so they could slip away unseen if needed. I stopped about ten feet from the tent.

"You have any sidearms hidden? We both have guns out in case you were to try anything."

"I have a 9mm on my ankle. I think I'll leave it there."

"That is a wise choice. We heard you wanted to talk to us."

'I do, if you know anything about Mike Vickers' business. I'm looking to find out who killed him and why."

"You trying to look into our business is not smart."

"I'm not trying to get into the specifics unless there is something he did that led to his death. What I think so far is Mike was flying in pot. As far as who he was working with and those details, I don't need them. Unless one of his partners killed him."

"We did not kill him. I'll tell you what we know and some of what we think. But that is all. We don't want to be involved any more with this business."

"That is good with me."

"Some people Mike used to know from military service are here in the area. We met up from time to time, then ended up hunting together. We came to Hamilton County as he knew people and could get hunting leases. Sitting in deer camp, we got the idea to buy some pot legally, then sell it places where it was not as legal for recreational use. Seemed safe buying from legit growers. Just a side business was all. But it got big, fast. Mike decided flying it in was the safest way to bring it. But then it got too big. We started spending a lot of our time weighing and packing, and the volume was too big to get rid of easily. The margins were not great either since we were paying a premium for legal pot; then we had to lower prices to wholesale levels in order to sell it bulk to other distributors. To make good money, we needed to sell it ourselves, but we didn't have the distribution network. Because none of us signed up to be dealers, we didn't want to do it anymore. We decided to quit and the whole thing ended weeks ago."

"Did Mike quit when everyone else did?"

"Our business was over, but Mike wanted to keep flying. It was the only way he could make enough money to keep his plane and pay for flying. He knew there was another outfit around, and one night he came to talk to us. He was trying not to act scared, but he was because he had found the other pot crew and went to offer his services."

"I assume it didn't go well."

"He said they laughed at him. Told him something about he was the wrong kind of pilot for the transport they used in their operation. Then they got mean and threatened him, and he left. After that, cars started following him around."

"Did he know who they were?"

"It was pretty obvious since they were Hamilton County Sheriff's cars."

"Anything happen after that?"

"Yeah, a week later he was dead. We got the message loud and clear even though we were already done with the pot business. Already we dropped the hunting leases up here and won't be back. We probably should not even be here talking to you."

"I'm glad you are. But what he said about being told he was the wrong kind of pilot. Any idea what that meant?"

"No, but we talked about it after Mike was killed. In case we needed to track them down and send them a message if they came after us. But we don't know what it meant."

"Which was stupid to even think about," said a second, female voice. "Even though they should be hunted down."

"Last thing," I said. "Were the sheriff's cars tailing Mike because the other gang tipped the sheriff off, or was the sheriff the other gang?"

"We don't know. But either way, we are gone from here. Too much potential for trouble. You keep asking around and you'll find it too."

"Thanks for the talk. Now I'm going to walk out of here."

"Good luck finding who did it. But you already know how dangerous they are."

"I do."

"If you are not working with the police and need some armed backup, get back in touch. We are not above some payback. But we don't intend to go up against the law. At least the real ones."

"I understand. Thanks again."

I began walking back to my car.

"Bryan, did you get all of that?" I said to my phone.

"Yes, I did. Things are getting interesting around here."

"Yes, they are. I'm going to leave my phone on until I get back to the house. I don't think they will do anything, but I see no reason to take any chances."

"Good idea. Just no funny noises on the way, please."

"Ten-four."

While I walked, I searched for the word "pilot" on my phone. Someone who operates a plane, spaceship, or boat was generally what I saw. I had a hunch it wasn't a spaceship bringing in pot. But that left a boat or ship. That was a neat trick, since there was not a navigable river or waterway in Hamilton County. What did it mean?

The other important part was the Hamilton County Sheriff was all over this, whether as an enforcer for the pot crew, or maybe he was the boss. Bryan was going to have to deal with that part, either with the state police, the DEA, or both. The sheriff had too much power in the county to take on without backup. I decided I needed a plan to deal with the sheriff when he came for me. Maybe it would not happen, but it was smarter to assume he would at least threaten me.

When I got to Warm Springs, I told Bryan I had an errand to do and we ended the call. I needed to do something I probably should have already done. Donna picked up on the second ring.

"Hey James.

"Hey Donna.

"What are you up to?"

"Uh, well, that is a long story. One that I'd like to tell you about when you have time."

"That sounds ominous. Is something wrong?"

"Not exactly, at least not yet. You know about the murder investigation where I've been working with the Warm Springs Campus Police. It has gotten complicated, and I think I need someone to talk through it. But only if you want to."

"I would like to hear about it, especially if it will keep you out of trouble. I can meet you in half an hour if you are in town."

"Thanks Donna. Do you want to come to my house or meet somewhere, maybe Mable's or the bookstore?"

"The bookstore. We can talk in private if you close it for a while. And you can get me a slice of pie from Mable's as payment."

"I like the way you think. See you there."

I parked at the store and waited for Donna. She walked in and I put up the Closed sign. She gave me a quick kiss, which I took as a good sign. We sat down, and I told her the entire story with details. Bryan might not have been happy, but I needed to talk, both to get my story worked out and to get another person's opinion. Donna listened graciously and asked pertinent questions. It took me about thirty minutes to get everything out, including what I had experienced today.

"This isn't just you telling me about the case," Donna said after I finished. "You are warning me something bad could happen."

"I don't think so, but if the sheriff is involved, I'm worried about what he might do. He does have a lot of power in the county, and has a lot to lose if he gets investigated."

"I'm not worried. Did you know we were cousins? He won't do anything to me."

"I, uh, what? You are cousins with General Custer?"

She laughed. "I like that name. Most people call him a lot worse. But yes, we are cousins. We are not close because I don't like him and never have. But I'm close with his mom. She might be the only person he listens to."

"I can't believe I told you all this, and he's your relative."

"It's OK, James. I'm not telling him. And knowing him, everything you said is true. If so, it needs to come out. He's a big boy and if he's playing on the other side, he needs to go to prison. We all thought he would be a contractor, then go to jail for fraud or tax evasion. Nobody in the family thought he would be sheriff. But looks like he will still end up where we all thought he would."

"Well then, that makes me feel better. I thought this was about to go sideways."

"No reason for it to. Besides, I like a good mystery. But it feels kind of yucky knowing someone got murdered, maybe because of something Jeffers is into."

"Jeffers? Never heard the sheriff called that."

"Only the family uses it."

"Did you gain an appetite for pie from my story?"

"I did and your treat, remember?"

"Are you ready to be seen in public with me? Once we walk next door together, the town will start talking."

"James, they already are. I even started some of it. That is how we do things around here. Come on and take my arm, escort me to the awaiting pie."

"Yes, my dear."

We calmly walked together into the bright sunlight, then into the coolness of Mable's. The hum of conversation dimmed a little with our entrance. Lottie even cracked a hint of a smile from behind the counter. I guess it was official.

CHAPTER EIGHTEEN

"You think Mike Vickers was piloting a plane full of marijuana once a week?" Donna asked a day later.

"I think so. That is what might have gotten him killed."

"That requires you to do research on the airports and planes around the area. You will have a much better idea of what he might have been doing."

"A very good idea. I'll visit the local airports, see the planes, possibly even talk to people working there or the pilots based there."

"You also need to charter and plane and fly around the area. Get a better feel for it."

"I would rather be dragged by the leg through a cactus patch by a donkey. Small planes make me nervous."

"Give it a chance, you might love it. I'll go with you."

"Ah, I figured it out. You love to fly and you goaded me right into this conversation, didn't you?"

"I do like the thrill of small planes. Not going to hold that against me, are you?"

"No, but now I know you have a crazy bone floating around somewhere in that skeleton."

"If I do, it is up to you to find it," she said teasingly.

"Perhaps the coroner will find it if there is anything left of us after the small plane crash."

"Psshh. Such a pessimist. We will probably survive one flight."

"I love the word 'probably' in that sentence."

"I should get my pilot's license. We can take a Cessna up and join the mile-high club."

"Donna, you just combined one of my favorite things to do with one of my least favorite things. I might be scarred for life."

"You'll get over it. Now let's drive over to the local airports."

It was not a long drive to either. The first one, the Roosevelt airport, was on the north side of Warm Springs. The Pine Mountain airport, surprisingly, was in Pine Mountain. It was larger than Roosevelt and had service for small jets. Probably for the corporate people flying important guests and customers to the Pine Gardens Resort. At both I found and wrote down numbers of the airport and charter services.

I decided to try Roosevelt first, while we were still in Pine Mountain. I called the airport thinking it was small enough that nobody would answer. But someone did. I explained that I was looking for a short charter flight for two people around Warm Springs. They told me they would check and call me back. I felt like luck was not running in my direction. I was proven right a few minutes later when my phone rang. A plane was available today if we could get there. I said yes, and they told me which hangar and pilot to look for. Donna was thrilled; me, not so much.

I drove to the other airport while Donna assured me it would be fun. The correct hangar was easy to spot, as there were only two and a man was standing in front of one and waving at us. We got out and met the pilot. His name was Glenn, we learned after introductions. Donna asked him if he was local.

"I typically fly in and out of Newnan," Glenn said. "I'm only here today because a client wanted me to fly him around his hunting estate so he could get pictures yesterday. Tomorrow I'm flying his guests back to Atlanta after they finish playing golf at Pine Gardens. I fly over there, pick them up, ferry them, and be back at my house in Newnan in about three hours. It is good money for something I love to do."

Glenn the pilot seemed nice enough. I wanted to ask him how much life insurance he carried but thought it might be in bad taste. He seemed more interested in talking to Donna than me. Perhaps because she was more interested in what he had to say about the plane and flight. Or because she was more attractive than me. Either way, I didn't have to listen or talk much. That gave me more time to worry about falling out of the sky. I vaguely heard something about flying at 5000 feet altitude, and the projected route at our airspeed would take about 45 minutes. I nodded occasionally to show I was actively involved in the process. Finally, I realized I was here to get something to use for my Vickers investigation.

"Glenn, what is your schedule like for this area?" I asked. "Are you busy dealing with people like us all year?"

"Spring can be a little slow. Summer picks up due to the tourist season, with people wanting to see Pine Mountain or their farms. Fall is my best season. I fly a lot of hunters around, plus there are lots of people flying to college football games."

"This airport seems a little slow and empty. Does it have all the accommodations you and your plane need?"

"It does. About all I need is fuel, a pilot's lounge, and a hangar for overnight heavy weather cover for the plane. It's all here, although getting the fuel can be a little slow at times. Are you guys ready to fly?"

Donna gave an enthusiastic yes. I complied with a noncommittal nod.

"I need to make a last check inside," Glenn said. "You guys can check out the passenger seats or walk around the plane. Just don't get into or touch anything in the cockpit."

"Thanks."

"James, why don't you like small planes?" Donna asked.

"Honestly, I've never been in one this small."

"Why the reluctance then?"

"Early in my career I worked for a company based in Arkansas and Oklahoma. We had a cute little airport in town with exactly two gates. Two airlines offered flights on prop planes that had 12 seats."

"That sounds lovely."

"I took a lot of flights around the Midwest and the South-Central region. Places like Dallas, Memphis, Oklahoma City, Kansas City, and Atlanta. In the winter, we flew into lots of severe storms with ice; summers, we were in massive thunderstorms. The kind with hail, tornadoes, and wind shear. A number of flights were punctuated by synchronized puking. It's hard to describe how bad those flights were unless you've been on them."

"That sounds bad. I guess you are still traumatized by them. But look at the sky, it is perfect weather today."

"That is the only reason I'm still standing here rather than running and shrieking across the runway to the car."

"Oh, come on, it will be fine. You get to sit beside me and I'll hold your hand. And I promise, no puking."

"OK, fine, I'll be good. Maybe Glenn will be back from the bathroom soon."

"I see him coming now. We will be off the ground in a few minutes and you'll see how fun it is."

Glenn came to the plane, and we all got in. It was slightly larger inside than I expected. Donna and I sat side by side behind Glenn, and there was an empty seat beside him. Behind us, I could see one jump seat and an empty space for cargo. Glenn told us more about the plane and its capability. I paid attention this time as it might be important to know what Vickers dealt with.

"Glenn, how much cargo can a plane like this carry?" I asked.

"Theoretically about 2000 pounds, but I'd never fly that weight. Depends on a lot of factors. Passengers, headwinds, speed and distance, if the cargo is balanced, those kinds of things. I prefer not to fly any weight over 1400 pounds. Planes and pilots are different, but that is the sweet spot for me and this plane. Today, with just us, this thing will take off like a dandelion puff. Even with the heavy air."

"What is heavy air?"

"Warm air holds moisture and is heavier. Takes a few more feet on the runway to get off the ground. A clear, sunny day like this in the winter with no humidity, and this plane will need a hundred feet less of runway. It'll pop off the ground."

The engines came on and it got loud, so a good time to end the chatting. He did a lot of piloting things while Donna and I made small talk, since we were so close and could hear each other.

"OK, we are taxiing out and will be in the air in two minutes," Glenn said loudly. And we were.

The airport was straight north of Warm Springs, so we went south and gained altitude quickly. We circled the campus, then went west over the Vickers' property, then banking right and up to Durand. It was once a town, but now a sparse community. Then east and over to Woodbury. Banking right again, we went over the Cove. I got Glenn to circle it so we could get a better view. Even Donna thought it looked like a crater. Then we flew back west and stayed over the Pine Mountain ridge over to the town of Pine Mountain. As we went over Pine Gardens, we saw the golf courses and lakes which looked nice from up here. I could even see where I hit the golf ball into the lake. A sharp bank and we headed back to the Roosevelt airport. Landing was easy, and Glenn taxied the plane to back where we began. No turbulence, nausea, or death had occurred, so I deemed it a successful flight.

I had already given Glenn a credit card for payment, so he dropped us near the pilot lounge, then took the plane to a nearby hangar.

"James, despite all your anxiety, I believe you survived."

"I did. It was much better than anticipated."

"Did you learn anything?"

"While up there and looking down, I realized there is no way to find something like a storage container where they might be repacking pot. It's a rural area, lots of trees and farms, and impossible to find something like that unless you already knew where it was."

"I agree. Meanwhile, I was noticing how pretty the land was from the plane."

"It is nice. And the ride was nice."

"See, I knew you would like it if you tried it."

"Does that apply to my fellow passenger as well?"

"James, I do believe you have turned the tables and are now teasing me."

"Something like that. I'm not sure how much is teasing versus something more substantial."

"I think we are ready to talk about things."

"That sounds ominous."

"No, just practical. We should talk about what are we both thinking about regarding where this might go. And ideas on what that looks like in the short-term. That kind of stuff."

"Eminently practical, and I agree. We are old enough to discuss everything and I don't want to make a dumb mistake or wrong assumption."

"Exactly. We don't have to do that anymore. Should we go to your house and have that conversation?"

"I think so. Maybe have a little something in our iced tea and sit on the porch."

"I like the sound of that."

Apparently, the discussion went well. We agreed, like adults, to not be rash and rush into anything. No reason to go fast; rather, we should start with becoming good friends first. I think we were both proud of our maturity. In the morning, I woke up and went to the kitchen and made pancakes and coffee—for two. Kat roused from sleep and needed some breakfast and to be let out. I heard Donna stirring in the bedroom and bathroom. She came out wearing my robe.

"I hope what I am seeing and smelling is for breakfast," she said.

"It certainly is. Kat is already fed, so all these leftovers are ours."

"I see you have your priorities straight."

"I have to keep the lady of the house content. Otherwise, she might claw the drapes."

"We don't want the drapery injured."

Conversation trailed off as we ate. We both were eating and drinking orange juice with a vengeance. As the food dwindled, the conversation picked back up.

"James, I believe we did what we jointly agreed late yesterday that we would not do," Donna said.

"We did."

"Technically, it was our third date. Although if golf counts, it might have been the fourth."

"Did that magical number require our mutual disrobing?"

"It did not. But apparently it does for some people. What do we do now?"

"We continue with our agreement to not do anything like that while becoming better friends. Our logical discussion and decision still makes sense. But we forgive ourselves if we find ourselves breaking the agreement."

"I agree with that."

"Want to go shower with me?"

"I agree with that as well. Then we shall resume our agreement."

"I like all the agreement."

"Shut up and get in the shower."

CHAPTER NINETEEN

I was convinced Sheriff Jefferson Jackson, also known as J.J. or General Custer, was deep in the illegal pot business. Proving it would be much more difficult. Doing it without him knowing I did it was likely impossible. But I had to find out what I could to help put him away if necessary.

I pulled up the county property records. The sheriff lived in a nice brick ranch house of a little over 2000 square feet. There were two outbuildings shown on the records and map, with one being a garage. Although the house was not ostentatious, the property was. The house sat on a hundred and fifty acres. Approximately five acres wide at the road and thirty acres deep, in a rectangle shape. A pond was between the house and road, with woods on both sides of the pond and no close neighbors. The vast majority of the property was behind the house, and looked like rolling hills, mostly wooded with occasional clearings. They might be planted food plots to draw in deer for hunting. Otherwise, I didn't know of a reason for small clearings to be sprinkled in the woods like that.

I was hoping for more. A large X marking the spot where the illegal activities occurred would have been nice. Or a long grassy strip suitable for planes to land. But neither of those was on the map. I needed to see it for myself.

I drove to where he lived and found the house was off the highway but visible. I pulled off the road across from the driveway to take a fast look with binoculars. A brick ranch with a pond between it and the road, just like the county property map showed. The drive ran from the highway across the pond dam and to the side garage of the house. There was another detached garage to the side of the house and driveway. A new pickup sat near the house, along with a bright lime green car. I studied it through the binoculars and realized it was a late model Mustang. Just like the one Mike Vickers once owned, but a different color. Interesting but something to look into once the sheriff was arrested.

I could not see the second building from my vantage point. It was behind the house. I drove off, turned around, and slowly came back. A hundred yards away from his driveway was a pull in under the pine trees. It was an old logging access or abandoned driveway. There had been a cable across it to keep people like me out, but it was on the ground and the lock gone. I pulled in and could drive in deep enough to use the pines to shield my car from the road. I did not like the setting but did not intend to be here long.

I got out and walked through the trees toward the sheriff's house. I stopped when I was close enough to glimpse it through the lower limbs and brush. There was a building out behind the house, but looked like a large storage shed. A short flatbed trailer was parked near it. An excavator, medium-sized, was on the trailer along with three large yellow plastic containers with black lids. Each of them was probably six feet tall, three feet wide, and eight feet long. This might be part of a side business Sheriff J.J. was running, and possibly a way to launder money. Something I'd check into soon. I had seen enough and crept back to my car. I backed up out of the woods and onto the road.

Spying on the sheriff's house was dangerous, but I felt I had not been seen. Nothing obvious was there, but I wondered about the construction equipment and the green car. I was smart enough to know not to go back. Time to check in with my employer. Although I was not getting paid or receiving benefits, maybe Bryan could keep the sheriff from accidentally shooting me. Once on campus, I went to see him.

"Bryan, I drove out past the sheriff's house today."

"I'm not sure that is a good idea. You don't want to get his attention."

"One time and I won't go back. Do you know if the

sheriff has a side business? Something like putting in septic tanks for new construction?"

"I have not heard anything about it if he is. I ran some checks on him and there are no business licenses for him or his immediate family. I thought he might be using a side business to launder some money."

"I thought the same. While I was out there, I saw a trailer with an excavator and three septic tanks behind his house."

"He had a trailer of septic tanks? Big ones?"

"Yeah, each one of them was big enough for a large house. He must be working with someone putting in a subdivision."

"I'll take another look, but I don't think he has any businesses, much less septic tank installs."

"I need to take a close look as well. He must have some way of moving cash to recycle it back to himself through laundering. Or sending it to offshore accounts."

"He or someone would have to physically take the cash. It will be hard to catch him without getting lucky, as he might do it only a few times a year."

"I was thinking about that. Seems like if he has a secret and reliable pot import chain, he could send money out with it."

"That makes sense. Pot is bulky coming in, and that much cash would also be bulky going out. At least several duffel bags."

"Thinking about it logically, a good pot business would make him, what, 20 million a year after expenses?"

"Hard to say, but that is a reasonable guess."

"What would you do with it if it were you?"

"I suppose I would stash a bunch of money, maybe a few different places. In case I needed to make a bribe or run if I was about to get caught. After that, I guess it would go to offshore accounts. That would be the long-term money for retirement or maybe leaving the country to stay away from the IRS and DEA. What about you?"

"I would do the same. I would expect to get caught, eventually. Someone in the organization makes a mistake and gets caught or talks to the wrong person. Even if that does not happen, when you retire and start spending huge sums of money, if you are still in the US, you would be more likely to draw attention and get caught. Better to have a foreign destination set up or at least have the money there."

"I can picture old J.J. now sitting on a beach, his own beach probably, sipping a drink and thinking about how smart he was."

"Makes you mad, does it not?"

"It does. I think it is my duty to make sure it does not happen."

"Speaking of stashing a bunch of money around here, those septic tanks make me think he might not be in the septic install business."

"Definitely. I've heard of them being used as tornado shelters. Bury them and jump in when the sky turns dark green."

"Since they are waterproof, it would make a good place to store what you don't want people to see or know about. How many duffels would one of them hold? I bet quite a lot."

"I think we now know where some of the cash is. Now

it would be good to know how the rest gets transported and where it goes."

"I can try to check, but since you are official, you will have resources I don't."

"I'll need to be careful, but I have friends at the DEA and GBI to ask in an unofficial capacity. If it is official, somebody will eventually tell the sheriff."

"I saw something else out there that might be important or could be nothing. He has a lime green muscle car, looks like the same make and model as Mike Vickers. Except for the color, of course."

"Surely he is not that stupid. If Doyle stole it, painted it and sold or gave it to him, the sheriff would have to know where it came from."

"It is worth checking, anyway. If I see it in town, I'll try to get a photo of the VIN plate to check it."

"Again, be careful. But if it is Vickers' car, it will be easy to get a search warrant for the sheriff's property. If one of those septic tanks shows up, then he can't get out of it and goes to prison."

"Sounds easy, but I bet it doesn't happen that way."

"No, it won't. The sheriff knows the system as well as anybody in the state."

"Know anybody that might rat on him?"

"All the deputies are either loyal or scared of him. I suspect a lot of them are involved with the pot operation."

"If they are, at least one of them might be careless with their extra income."

"Possibly, but I expect the sheriff is watching them. Still, might be worth looking at the county records for personal property. If one has a new farm or a dozen cars, I can leverage that against them."

"I keep going back to what Vickers' buddies said about the other operation, in regard to a pilot. I think you should check the records for boat ownership as well. Who has multiple boats, or larger boats than usual around here? Maybe even look at helicopters. There has to be something to that comment."

"I will. Now you stay away from the sheriff unless you can get a look at the green car when he is not around."

"If I promised to, would you believe me?"

"Not at all."

"Donna told me she was cousins to General Custer."

"Poor Donna, I bet she doesn't tell that to many people."

"She definitely does not like him, which is a theme in the family. But she said she is close to his mother. So I'm wondering whether any family members might be worth talking to about him."

"Could be, but they probably won't. They may not like him, but it is a small town and most tend to not talk about family, regardless of how bad they are."

"I think you are right. But one more thing bothers me regarding Mike's murder. If he was out of the business because his partners bailed, then went to the other gang to talk, why would they kill him since he was no longer a competitor?"

"No reason to, unless they thought he was going to turn them in. Would have been grounds for intimidation, like following him around with sheriff's cars."

"That should have kept him quiet. But that removes the motivation to kill him."

"We probably won't have that answer until the pot gang gets arrested. Somebody will rat to get their sentence reduced."

"I'm sure you are right. Now I'm going home and plan to stop thinking about all this for a while."

CHAPTER TWENTY

D oyle Vickers had a reputation. It was not a good one and seemed to rival the sheriff's for dislike within the county. Lottie told me Doyle was banned from Mable's Diner for an incident with another customer. It was serious enough that Lottie brought out a double-barreled shotgun to encourage Doyle to leave. I bet that had not happened in town in a long time. Although my research related to the letter under the cottage had turned up an old newspaper account of one of the young male Bullochs, of the family which Bullochville was named after, had an altercation at the hotel in town. Young Bulloch pulled a gun and killed the hotel proprietor; before he died, the man took the gun away and shot Bulloch three times and killed him. Bullochville was the original name of the town of Warm Springs. Roosevelt had pushed to rename Bullochville to Warm Springs and was persuasive enough to get it done. That meant the shooting had occurred more than a hundred years ago in the building very near my bookstore.

I knew from the county records Doyle lived outside of Warm Springs on the western edge of town, along the road filled with the Vickers' family properties. Asking a few people around town about him, including Lottie, garnered me a lot of curse words. His towing business was a necessity, but not many people liked the owner. I rarely ran across a person so universally disliked. Except for me in certain academic circles. But it wasn't me, it was them. I went to Manchester first to visit his business property.

Doyle's towing business was on the edge of town. It was a large metal building set back from the highway. Four large metal bay doors went down one side, with one regular entrance door on the front of the building. There were no windows. An old asphalt drive filled the space between the road and the front of the building; the rest of the lot on both sides was gravel. Various wreckers in states of disrepair littered the gravel, interspersed with a few late model wrecked cars and trucks. Weeds sprang up from the gravel and all around the building. The entire lot was encircled by an eight-foot-tall chain-link fence topped with razor wire. An open gate was set across the asphalt drive. My first impression, and all others afterward, was that it was an eyesore. The owner had no regard for his own space or the town. I knew tow drivers had lots of free time between jobs, but apparently the operation of a weed eater was beyond their capacity or motivation. The only thing the place was missing were the cliched junkyard dogs. It was probably too much trouble to feed them.

Then I drove out to the west side of Warm Springs, where I had previously gone to see the Vickers' property. Doyle's house was not visible from the road. The only thing new I saw was a gate across one of the gravel roads. From what I could tell, it was the road back into the large lot with the lake on it. The gate was shiny, as were the hinges, so it was quite new.

I decided I needed to meet the famous Doyle. I could arrange an automobile emergency, but I was not sure whether Doyle or one of his men would be driving the tow truck. I scratched that idea. The problem was I could not think of another good way to do it. No way was I going to wreck a car just to meet him.

Maybe records could point me in the right direction for Doyle, and maybe the sheriff as well. I found Lottie in the diner before closing, as I knew I would. I sat at the counter but did not order. She looked at me and nodded. She would come over once the last customer was gone.

"Lottie, if I was buying up cars, boats, planes, and such, how could I do it and hide my ownership?"

"Hah, I knew you were crooked. You must be a bank robber looking to sock away his ill-gotten gains."

"Yeah, you got me. I'm a mastermind criminal."

"Not if you admit it. First of all, if you are looking up who I think you are, you need to be careful. If you do it in person at the courthouse, people are going to talk. You don't want that getting back to the wrong folks."

"True, so how do I do it?"

"You don't. Tell me what you are looking to find, and I can get into the system without any notice."

"OK, even so, how to hide property ownership?"

"Most use a corporation to show as the owner on the county records. Lately it has been LLCs. The smart ones have at least another one or two levels of corporate ownership above that, so individual names don't show up. Best you can do is go to the Secretary of State website and start ferreting out the corporate records. Even then, sometimes all you get is the registered agent. Usually a lawyer, and that is a dead end unless you get him to talk."

"Not likely."

"No, because if he's working for crooks, he won't give himself up. Now what are you looking for?"

"A couple of things. The sheriff has a new bright green car, a Mustang that I'm curious about. Also, anybody in the county with multiple boats. Not bass boats, but big expensive ones. Last, any airplanes, helicopters, expensive stuff."

"Not a problem to dig that up. You will have to chase down the corporate stuff though if it is listed that way."

"I can do that since I've done it before."

"Yeah, but what if these items are listed in another county?"

"Oh, that could be a problem."

"Nope, I can check the neighboring counties as well. But you are going to owe me."

"Bookstore discount?"

"A lot more than that. I'll come up with something appropriate."

"Thanks Lottie."

I was in the bookstore the next day when Lottie knocked on the door as she came in. "You decent in here?" she asked.

"Why in the world wouldn't I be? You must be thinking about the so-called bookstores you went to in your youth in New York City."

"You'd be surprised at some of the places I've been. But since you spend most of your time in here alone, without customers, I thought you might be walking around without your shirt on."

"This is not a clothing optional establishment, even for the owner. "

"Glad to hear it. Here is your list from the county. Not a lot, but should be enough to get you started. Five large boats are registered to a single company, an LLC, in Hamilton County. They are all large expensive boats you would expect to find in a coastal marina."

"Interesting since there are not even any lakes in the county large enough to keep these boats."

"I thought the same. Also found a plane registered to an LLC that I don't know. I suspect is the one you are looking for, since I can track down all the others listed. Nothing on the sheriff having a car recently."

"I appreciate this, Lottie. I assume you covered your tracks?"

"Of course, nobody even knows I was in the system. Easy enough since I set it up."

"What about land transfers? The county website is nearly a year behind updating the records."

"Sure, those are easy. What are you looking for?"

"Any sales or transfers with any of the Vickers family

properties. Or loans or liens, anything recent. Maybe take a look at the Jackson family properties as well."

"That will take me about five minutes."

"I'll stop by about closing time if you think you'll have it today."

"I will. See you later. Good luck."

I began searching the online site of the Secretary of State. I found the LLC that owned the boats. No individual company officers or owners were listed. The registered agent was Lawrence K. Endicott, IV. That was a name that would get you beaten up as a kid but accepted into most law schools later. A quick search showed he was a practicing lawyer in Hamilton, but little else.

I found the LLC which was shown as the owner of the plane. Again, no company officers or individual owners. The registered agent was Lawrence K. Endicott, IV. This guy got around in some interesting legal circles. But it did not prove he was a crook, since he could be the only lawyer in the county handling business registrations.

I closed the store early and went next door to see Lottie. They had just closed and she let me in.

"Here's your other list," she said. "Again, not much on it, but what is there you might find useful."

"Thanks again. Say, do you know Lawrence K Endicott, number four?"

"Mostly just by hearsay. He's a young fellow. Went to law school and later inherited a little money and property. Used to be called Larry the Lawless."

"Why, is he a crook?"

"No, not that I know about. He has a little office in Hamilton, but never does any lawyering. Sort of a trust fund attorney, one that likes being a lawyer but does not practice."

"He was the registered agent for two of those LLCs. Maybe he specializes in business registrations."

"Could be. Those go through the state so makes sense, since the county doesn't register them. Most lawyers do specialize in a field like litigation or family law. But I was surprised to see he was the closing attorney for the land transfer."

"What land transfer?"

"The recent one from Mike Vickers to Doyle Vickers. Two people you might be interested in."

"Very much so. I imagine that was the big parcel where the lake was located."

"It is. Dated a few days before Mike's body was found, but filed with the courthouse the day before he was found."

"That is not suspicious at all. Mike seemed like a quiet guy, but sure picked up some enemies."

"That would be apparent, considering he was murdered. I can see why you did not pursue a career in criminal justice."

"I did not have time since I was enrolled in Obvious School."

That got a snort from Lottie. "At least you can laugh at yourself. Might be up to Donna's standards, after all."

"I hope to live up to your level of confidence."

"You better. Otherwise you'll not have anybody teaching you to play golf."

"You've already heard about that. She did thrash me soundly."

"I bet she did. She was one of the best athletes in her county back in high school and later in college."

"I could tell, and I bet she still is. And I don't mind at all."

"Get out of here, Romeo, before you wax poetic and make me nauseous. I need to close up and go home."

CHAPTER TWENTY-ONE

I saw a car moving through Manchester just like the one I'd seen at the sheriff's house. A new model Mustang muscle car, a distinctive bright lime green color with a black stripe on the hood. Other than the color, it was just like people had described Mike Vickers' car. I was in Manchester picking up some items when I saw it. From a distance, it looked like the sheriff driving, but I could not be sure. On the chance it was him and he was in town for errands instead of passing through, I followed. I kept a healthy distance behind him. He pulled into a parking space in front of the hardware store. He got out, stood beside the car as he looked at himself in the reflection of the side window and adjusted his hat. It was definitely J. J., Sheriff Jackson.

He would likely be in the store for at least a few minutes, so I had time to park and take a closer look at the car. I parked a hundred feet away and walked up to the nauseatingly green vehicle. The store windows were so full of merchandise, the sheriff could not see me near his car.

I walked around it and leaned over the windshield. I noticed it had the racing harnesses inside instead of seat belts. Oddly, the metal plate displaying the Vehicle Identification Number was missing. I checked the side windows where the VIN was normally etched. None of the glass windows had the number, either. My mind was rapidly concluding the sheriff was driving a stolen car. As casually as I could, I moved away and walked back to my car.

The next day at the store, I heard the door of the shop open. Kat was off her perch and in the back like a shot, portending an unfriendly visit. The door did not shut immediately, so maybe more than one person. I excused myself from present company and stepped around the bookshelf to find out what fresh hell was in my store.

It was the sheriff and his favorite deputy. This was not going to go well.

"Sheriff and deputy," I said. "Is there something I can help you with?"

I got a menacing glare times two. I considered laughing out loud at the absurdity of a crooked lawman and his sidekick threatening me in a bookstore.

"I heard you have been looking into the recent murder of Mike Vickers. Playing lapdog to that jumped up campus cop."

"Despite your implied sneer, the description is accurate. Except for the lapdog part. That designation is reserved for your deputy."

"Hear that, Deacon? This citizen just insulted you. I'm not sure you have to take that from him. Perhaps you should remind him of his manners."

"I don't believe this shop is in your jurisdiction."

"That ain't gonna save you from the beating you deserve. We came in to ask questions and you became unruly, then you resisted arrest. The place got trashed, and you got knocked around. But not as much as you need. We'll finish that in my jail. You won't be asking any more questions about my business. We'll be nice and take that ratty cat to the pound on the way. Deacon, go ahead."

"Jeffers, you idiot," Donna said as she came around the bookshelf I had just left. It was like a floodlight had caught a raccoon in the trash can as Donna's words and presence sank in. "Do you really intend to cause James harm for no reason? With me standing here and watching?"

"Uh, Donna, I had no idea you were here."

"Obviously. Now what are you doing that you have to threaten people to keep quiet?"

"Uh, nothing. Nothing at all. This was just a misunderstanding, is all. Harmless fun. Deacon, let's go."

"Jeffers?"

"Yes Donna?"

"This won't be happening again."

"No, it won't." He was giving Donna the sheepish look, but as he went through the door, I got the menacing look again. I believe the man was unhappy with me.

"Donna, my hero," I said. "I believe I owe you my life and livelihood. Can I buy you a piece of pie?"

"You are not getting off that easy. This was worth at least another dinner."

"And breakfast after?"

"Totally dependent on how good the dinner is."

"Despite what he said, you know this is not over."

"That is what he thinks. I saw him give you that look as he left. I'll be talking to his mom and a few others. But all he did today was reinforce both everything I already knew about him and what you've told me."

"He's dirty and mean."

"Yes. But is he a murderer?"

"I don't know yet. But he's in my top two suspects."

"He's worse than I thought. Very disappointing."

"I believe he nearly wet himself when you showed up. You must have terrorized him as a child."

"Well, not much. When I babysat him, he got all mouthy and started trash talking. I put him in his place. Then his momma got ahold of him later. After a few times, he smartened up enough to not push me."

"Seems he learned nothing other than to hide his bad behavior."

"Apparently."

"You backed him down easily enough."

"I did. But I also recorded it in case he didn't comply."

"Oh, I like that."

"I'm sure it will come in handy for one or both of us. Now when is our next dinner date? And do you have a chocolate cake recipe ready to go yet?"

"Not yet. I'm embarrassed to say I've never made a chocolate cake."

"I'm aghast."

"Maybe we could make one together. You be there to show me how to make her recipe."

"I see the logic in that. Do you promise to behave yourself since we will be cooped up in your kitchen?"

"I do not. But I will promise it will be fun. Perhaps even a good cake will come out of it."

"I'm willing to try. James, had I not been at your shop today, what would have happened?"

"Probably something ugly. But it would not have lasted long."

"Why do you say that?"

"I have an emergency text code set up with Bryan. It goes to him and his force. I'd have texted it before walking out to meet Sheriff J.J. and Deputy Deacon if you had not been there. Bryan and company would have been at the shop within a minute or two."

"That is smart. You've been expecting it to happen, haven't you?"

"It was just a matter of time."

"I'm glad it didn't get ugly."

"Me too, and I appreciate your help. I hope it didn't make you a target."

"No, it did not. But wait, why didn't you text Bryan today?"

"I did. I was stalling a bit before you came out from the bookshelf. Then I reached in my pocket and canceled it."

"You were that sure of me?

"Yes, plus I had backup just in case."

"What kind?"

"I had an illegal taser in my other pocket. Deacon would have gotten a surprise, and a headache when he woke up."

"That would be little consolation if Jeffers had shot you."

"I thought the same thing. I was hoping Jeffers would have been alone. Since he was not, I texted and stalled. Then you saved me and I'm forever in your debt."

"Jeffers is worse than I thought. He is into something criminal, otherwise he wouldn't have threatened you."

"I share your conclusion. I'm a little worried about you being in my presence until this gets worked out."

"You mean until he's shot or arrested?"

"Yes, and either one works for me."

"I'm not going to let him deter me from doing anything. Don't you let him either, when it comes to me."

"Yes ma'am."

"That's better. Now tell me the truth. You did not have a taser in your pocket, did you?"

"No, I did not."

"What was it? A small automatic, like a .32 caliber?"

"Better. A hybrid double-to-single stack 9 mm. I think they call it a bookstore owner's special."

"I like that and I want to see it sometime. We can go to the range together."

"Sounds like another date."

"You bet it is."

After Donna left, I went home. My mind kept replaying the incident at the store. It could have gone bad, and quickly. The hidden camera would have given Bryan plenty of evidence to pursue a case, but it would not have saved me if shooting started and I didn't get them first. I needed to let Bryan know what happened. Plus, I now needed to get the sheriff put away and soon before he came after me again.

I walked next door to Bryan's office, even though it was late. His car was still out front. I knocked and went in.

"Hey Bryan, don't you ever go home early?"

"Not since Vickers' body showed up. Trish has been understanding so far, but her patience will run out. What are you doing at my office after dark? Brought me a nice dinner?"

"I could lie and say yes, but the evidence that I brought nothing would give me away. I wanted to let you know I had a visit from General Custer and Deputy Goon today."

"How did that go? I don't see any bruises."

"It was at the bookstore, and about to escalate to an OK Corral level, when Donna walked up and defused the whole thing. Turns out she is his older cousin and former babysitter. Somehow she still makes him mind."

"That sounds scary, but I would have loved to have seen it. Why didn't you text?"

"I was going to, but I had my other hand on backup. But I lied and told Donna I did text and then canceled."

"You should have texted, anyway."

"I know. I won't take that chance again."

"Maybe he knows about you looking at his car. Are you good enough with that little gun to take both of them?"

"One for sure. Fifty-fifty on the second. The camera would have given you what you needed to put him away.

But Bryan, I'm telling you all this because it was a couple of seconds away from going bad. I'm going to have flashbacks for a while and don't want it to happen again."

"That is good thinking, but you know if he did it once he'll try again. Next time, he will be smarter."

"I know. Donna thinks she is safe, but I don't trust him. I need to get him, and quickly."

"I second that motion. But we, or rather I, don't have much to proceed with a solid investigation."

"How about something a little less robust than a drug or murder investigation?"

"What do you mean?"

"His whole operation must be cash-based. So where does it all go? I intend to follow the money and at the very least get him for tax evasion. But I bet the cash trail will also implicate him for the drug business."

"That sounds great. What is your plan?"

"I don't have one yet. But there has to be something."

"I look forward to whatever you come up with. But the problem with law enforcement is often we have about 75 percent of what we need. Enough to know who did what. But we need closer to 95 percent to take action like arrests and search warrants. Probably 100 percent when we go after the sheriff."

"I know, I just don't like it. But if you know any way to find out his financial information, maybe I can use it to get to him, even without the pot angle. Another thought is to find his cash carriers. Could even be Doyle if he trusts him."

"I'm betting he only has one or two people he trusts to carry it."

"I think the same thing. Anyway, that is the beginning of my plan. I'll have more soon."

"You go think more about it. I'm going home."

185

CHAPTER TWENTY-TWO

Business at the store was slow, so I went next door to pick up some lunch. It was also a good place to find some extra information. There were some new small tables on the sidewalk, set up for two people. I tried one since nobody else was outside. It might have been because there was little shade and summer was coming early, but I'd chance it.

"You out here working on your tan now that you got a girlfriend Romeo?" Lottie asked when she came out.

"No, just wanted to make you come out here. I wanted to see if you would burst into flames."

"That is a myth. Vampires have no fear of the sun. Politicians have been proving that for years."

"I guess they have. Today I think I'll do the special."

"I'll go get it. Surprised you didn't order the steak."

"Oh, I see what you did there."

"I'm surprised you did. Next time you insinuate I'm a vampire, you'll get extra garlic in your tea."

Lottie left me to bake on the sidewalk. In about forty-five minutes, someone was going to stick a toothpick in me to see if I was done. I realized why I was alone out here. Mable's really needed to invest in some umbrellas. Lottie brought out my food but didn't stick around. I think she smirked at my sweatiness.

Millard went by in his mature go-cart. He waved and blew the anemic horn as Lottie came back out to get my dishes. He must be on his way to meet up with his card-playing buddies.

"I can't believe you gave Millard that contraption. He wants me to go for rides in it with him."

"That is sweet. You should say yes."

"You should know better than to tell me to say yes. That thing blows my hair to pieces."

"Not literally, I hope. Besides, I thought it was a wig."

"Are you being especially obtuse today?"

"Only if it is working to tease you."

"Keep it up, I'll stab you with a fork."

"Sounds like you've already been riding around with him."

"What do you want? The faster I get your dessert here the better chance you'll stop talking. Otherwise, I'll toss you out and give your spot to a compliant, paying customer."

"I'll take the banana pudding. No whipped cream. You

know I can get side doors for that thing. Then you won't have to worry about your hair."

"I'm going back in now to find a big serving fork. It will do more damage than these little ones."

"Can you bring me some sunblock?"

"Yeah, soon as I find some Elmer's glue to put in it."

I could see her point. The glue looked like sunblock. But the aftereffects were quite different. I gave up the sun torture and walked inside. The air conditioning felt wonderful as I took a seat at the counter.

Lottie came by with another smirk. I checked, but did not see her carrying a large fork or a bottle of glue. "You look like a wilted baked Alaska," she said.

"I feel like one. Might need some umbrellas out there."

"Can't do it. They are too much of a liability. They fall over, or the wind picks them up and drops them on customers. All kinds of things can happen."

"I guess the outdoor dining will be best utilized in the cooler months."

"Obviously. Well, for everybody except you."

"Lottie, do you know anything about a guy on the other side of the ridge buying up old chicken houses?" I did not tell her that Sam had already given me information about the same person, the alleged indoor pot grower.

"Of course I do. Why, you going to invest and become the next fried chicken king?"

"I'll take a hard pass on that option. I've heard he's running a business and figured you might know what it is."

"He has bought a few farms for cheap. Converting them to grow houses for sprouts and herbs and such. High end produce he ships to California."

"That is interesting. Not sure it makes the most sense from a shipping standpoint."

"It only does if the margins are high."

"From what I know about chicken houses, they can be converted to grow most anything."

"That they can. All kinds of things. Not all things grown need to be shipped to the West Coast."

"I think I'll go visit."

"Stop by the drug store and get you some calamine lotion for that sunburn on the way."

As I left Mable's, Millard came by, going the other direction. I flagged him down. The vest of the day was fuchsia.

"Hey Millard. You know anything about a computer guy from out west buying up old chicken houses in the south part of the county? I believe you referenced that in the report. I think I need to take a look at him."

"I heard a few things. He is young and has no family. From South Africa by way of England and California. Made a lot of money in tech startups."

"Ah, the Commonwealth Computer Mafia."

"Whatever. He's been around here the past year or so. Bought up some of those chicken farms after the company closed down."

"I guess he got them cheap."

"I don't think the money matters. He has one of those little jets over at the Pine Mountain airport."

"That's not cheap."

"Nope. He drives one of those electric trucks around here. Seems incongruous, if you ask me."

"What? How?"

"Flits about in a private jet yet drives what is supposed to be an environmentally friendly vehicle."

"I don't know. It makes some sense from a marketing perspective. People think it is environmental friendly. But in reality, those vehicles are not exactly efficient, nor the jet."

"So, it's a sham like most rich people things."

"In this case, yeah. Thanks for letting me know."

"No problem. You know those houses can grow all kinds of things, whether legal or not. We believe he's growing marijuana."

"That's why I'm going down to see him."

On my computer it took effort to find contact information for the boy genius. Almost as if he wanted to be known but not contacted. I suppose that was the newest fad for the crowd he was with. I wanted an appointment rather than showing up unannounced. A number was listed on the website, where a recorded message told me all about the wonderful company when I called. I left a message and surprisingly received a call an hour later. A woman's voice set up an appointment for later in the day and provided directions to meet Kapp Hendriks at one of his growing houses. To get the appointment, I might have exaggerated somewhat about my journalism credentials and wanting to highlight the Hamilton County operations.

My research found he was wealthy and had recently moved from Silicon Valley to run a hydroponics business. High end sprouts and greens to supply gourmet restaurants and shops in California. He had bought several of the old chicken farms that had houses in good shape after the processing plant closed down. The houses were fifty feet wide and four hundred feet long. All the space inside was open, even the rafter space overhead. It was perfect for a hydroponic operation. And plenty of other things, since each house had twenty thousand square feet of space.

The meeting spot was a cleaned-up farm with two newly painted chicken houses. A small house was also spruced up and I suppose it was headquarters, at least for the press and invited venture capitalists. A younger man was standing beside a Range Rover. He was wearing nice jeans, a sports coat, and rose-tinted sunglasses. I had not seen those in a while. His hair was in a ponytail.

I got out, and we shook hands. "I thought you drove an electric truck," I said. "The pictures were on the website."

"It is in the shop for some minor updates. This vehicle gives me the privilege to pay gas taxes, like so many others in this country."

"I appreciate your patriotism."

"Thank you. Let's take a peek inside the grow house. We can't go in as I'm promoting a clean environment and don't want to introduce any contaminants."

We looked in and I saw a typical hydroponics setup. Racks of green plants with roots in plastic water troughs. Lots of pipes and tubing to route the water. He closed the door rather quickly. I guess he did not want me to see too much.

"We have two different hydroponic systems," Kapp said. "One is the traditional system where we grow plants rooted in water."

"I am familiar with the system."

"We produce a variety of fresh leafy produce and

sprouts for customers in demographic areas with higher disposable income. We even have a line of microgreens."

"I assume you target the northeast and west coast markets."

"Yes, but mostly west coast. The other system is more complex because we are also producing protein."

"How is that? Are you growing beans?"

"A good guess, but no. It is an aquaponic system. The simple explanation is we use water to grow tilapia fish, and the water with the fish waste as fertilizer is pumped over to nourish the plant roots, then filtered and sent back to the tilapia tanks."

"That is an elegant system. But it sounds like a difficult one to manage."

"It is true, so we have experts to set it up. Then we use artificial intelligence to manage the daily operations and production system."

I nodded agreement, while thinking the guy was an idiot, a liar, or both. People could use computer systems to make decisions based on data inputs from monitors and prior data analyses. It was done everywhere with good results. But nobody would use AI alone to run a complex agricultural system. Especially not with fish, one of the most difficult commodities to produce in a closed system. It was like asking a nuclear physicist in the UK to manage a timber farm in Sri Lanka. But if it was really true, the guy was an absolute genius. Either way, why was he in rural Hamilton County, Georgia?

"Where is the tilapia processed?"

"Oh, we are still working on the white space encompassing the production paradigm. We envision scaling up the old chicken plant as an option to reopen with the right tax incentives. We are talking to a catfish processor in Alabama for now."

That was a fancy way of saying they were not processing any tilapia. But he was angling for a tax break at the old plant. I had seen the same thing with Russian investors in chickens. After the investment funds arrived, first the money disappeared, then the Russians.

"We also have a cooperative working agreement with the National Fish Hatchery in Warm Springs. We will implement best practices in tilapia management and disease mediation systems."

That was a nice way to say he had dangled some dollars in front of the feds, probably as a grant, to get them to sign on to some nebulous project that had not happened yet. But it gave Kapp some unearned credibility. Perhaps I was cynical, but I had seen just about every scam in the realm of agricultural research. The aquaponic operation sounded like a scam. But I needed to gush like I believed every word.

"Kapp, your systems sound incredible. I've never heard anything so innovative. I imagine you already have investors lined up to blow this into the next huge agricultural movement." Compliments were manna to narcissists.

"We have an impressive portfolio of investment groups, all top performing venture capitalists. Funding has not been an issue."

"Do you have other innovative business interests you've begun or have in development?"

"Our newest project is entofarming. Are you familiar with the term?"

I was, but I needed to play dumb. "It sounds familiar, but I don't remember what it is."

"We have a lot of spare capacity in the growout houses. To maximize the space and minimize energy inputs by utilizing the climate conditions, we are producing insects. Our first foray is growing crickets and worms."

"For human food or animal feed?"

"Good question. We feel we have the capability for a superior product and so we plan to serve the human market. Mostly through wholesale bulk powders. Animal feed requires less control and a lower quality product."

"Less profitable as well."

"Much less."

"I suppose you could supplement the tilapia diet."

"Another reason for entofarming. We like the synergy of all the circular production units. Each directly or indirectly feeds each other in the production system, producing healthy, sustainable products for premium markets."

More MBA-babble centered around rationalizing the consumption of fish bait and being proud of it. At least proud of it for long enough to charm some committee members and get a grant, investment, or tax break.

"The fish eat the bugs, fish poop and feed the plant roots, plants feed the bugs. And at times, some fish, plants, and bugs are pulled from the system to feed humans."

"I believe you have captured a synopsis of our operation."

"Oh, I forgot the profit extracted from the humans."

"That is a nice byproduct of the system. I daresay

feeding humans nutritious products outweighs matters of profit."

"That is a noble pursuit. How much is the retail price for the tilapia?"

"We sell to the finest establishments that prefer to provide their customers the utmost in both quality and sustainable premier items. The tilapia averages thirty dollars a pound."

"Definitely premier." Of course, wholesale tilapia was about two dollars a pound. His premier experience was all about marketing a mediocre protein to clients more concerned with appearance than anything else.

"We like to think so."

"I appreciate your time. I think I have everything I need for a writeup." One that would never happen.

Traditional gardening was not always drudge work. Sometimes you got to enjoy the fruits of your labors, literally. Or like today, we got to enjoy the vegetables of our labors. I closed up the bookstore, went home, and then to the garden. After planting sweet potatoes, we picked greens and pulled up carrots and radishes. We also cut some broccoli we had grown as a trial. Once we had everything harvested, we gave the bulk of it to George for use in the cafeteria. Since everything had to be cooked, all of it would go toward stir fry Wednesday. We divvied up the rest and traded some things around. I was not a carrot person, so I traded mine to Ernie for more radishes. We did not have the restrictions the cafeteria did, where produce was required to be cooked, so we all were looking forward to great salads. We were also looking forward to the next week as the peas should be ready and continue producing until hot weather.

As we moved toward the parking lot, Alisha came up to talk. "James, I wanted to ask you something."

"Sure, go ahead," I said.

"I know you are helping Bryan look at the Vickers case. I know somebody that might help if you want to talk to them."

"Thanks Alisha, I appreciate that. I would like to talk to them."

"Did you know that I'm kin to the Vickers on my mama's side?"

"No, I had no idea."

"I guess nearly everyone around here is kin to half of everybody else. Anyway, Doyle's wife, or I guess more of an ex-wife right now, could tell you a lot about the Vickers' family. Maybe not specifics on anything, but if nothing else, you would have more of an idea of the Vickers' family dynamics."

"That sounds good, Alisha. Should I call her?"

"No, probably not a good idea. You don't want to do anything that might get Doyle angry. He might find out somehow. I'll talk to her and maybe we can meet up somewhere out of town. She'd be more likely to talk."

"OK, you set it up. I can talk to her somewhere like Pine Gardens or up on Pine Mountain in the state park. Unless Doyle hangs around those places."

"I think something like that she would go along with. I'll call you when I know something."

"Thank you. Just let me know."

I took my veggies home, rinsed them off and once bagged, I put them in the refrigerator. I saw Bryan's car next door and walked over. He was just coming out to go home, so I would not keep him long.

"Hey Bryan. Got a minute? Really, not any longer."

"Sure, what you got?"

"I'm working on a meetup with Doyle Vickers' wife, or ex-wife. Can you think of any questions I should ask?"

"Maybe something about what in the world she was thinking, marrying him twice. Vicky's a bit rough, but I know she is smarter than that."

"Wait, her name is Vicky? Vicky Vickers. Surely you are kidding."

"Yep, that is her. She married the guy and took his name. She couldn't claim she didn't know what she was doing, especially the second time."

"OK then. What should I ask her?"

"Get right to it. Ask her if Doyle killed Mike. Could save me a lot of late dinners with Trish."

"That would cut to the chase. But it might circumvent your awesome detective powers."

"At this point, circumvent away. I'm hoping I can soon put my detective powers in the closet with my winter clothes and not need them again."

"I'll do what I can."

"All I can tell you is do it so that Doyle knows nothing about it. Safer for both of you."

"Yeah, Alisha already warned me. We will talk when and where Doyle won't know."

"Good. Let me know if you find out anything interesting."

"I will, goodnight."

Alisha called me the next morning with the news that Vicky would talk to me. We decided to meet at the top of Pine Mountain at one of the state park sites, Dowdell Knob. It was reputed to be one of FDR's favorite lookout spots. Alisha was coming with Vicky, so Doyle would not be suspicious. Doyle was more and more sounding like a prime suspect. I met them in the late afternoon in the parking lot. We sat at a picnic table not far from the small parking lot. Alisha made the brief introductions, then we began.

"Alisha tells me you are looking for information on folks, including Doyle," Vicky began. "I can tell you some things, but I have to be careful it doesn't get back to him where it came from."

"I can keep most anything quiet unless you tell me you have proof he's guilty of murder or similar."

"I can't tell you that because I don't know he's done anything like that."

"That's OK. What is your situation with Doyle right now?"

"We are divorced, or in the process for the second time. There won't be a third time. Although there just might be a funeral to celebrate. His, I hope. I like him less and less."

"Has he been violent toward you or other family?"

"Lots of threats to me and most everybody else. I know he has smacked people around. But usually tow customers he has ripped off from out of state, folks he knows he can slap and get away with it."

"It is still assault. Nobody files charges?"

"If they do, it drags on and gets dropped. The sheriff never gets around to investigating."

"But he has not hit you?"

"No. But I would not want to antagonize him too much. I believe he would if I pushed him. One reason I need to be careful talking to you. Another reason is he still owes me money or will after the divorce. If I go talking to you and he gets in trouble, I won't ever see it."

"Are you still on the deed to the house and property here in town?"

"I am. He will owe me for that, at least. Or half the value."

"If he has committed crimes at his business or elsewhere and goes to jail, but did not involve the house or property, you might get everything. Instead of half after the divorce."

"That sounds wonderful, if it happens. He's dirty as a snake, but never did anything at the house or around it. He was always going on about that being his sanctuary, and why he deserved all the land. Only he could take care of it. He nearly died when Mike got the land. Swore he would get it back if it was the last thing he did."

"I heard he got it back just before Mike was killed."

"I have not heard that. But if he could have, he did. Makes me wonder about poor Mike."

"Do you know anything about Doyle's business?"

"Just that he tows and steals everything in the cars he gets. Between the time he picks them up and then delivers, everything gets gone. The stereos, the wheels, catalytic converters, even seats and engines if he thinks it has value and he can move it quick."

"He has all that stuff in his Manchester building?"

"Oh no, that is his real business. He'd never put stolen stuff there."

"Where do the stolen items end up?"

"He got all smart and has a place nobody knows about between here and Interstate 85. He takes those cars off the highway after a wreck, takes them to that place and strips them. Then tows them on over to his official business in Manchester like there is nothing going on."

"Do you know where that place is?"

"Yeah, it's over along Highway 18, between I-85 and 185. He can work both interstates from there. Some kind of old building, like a former church or warehouse. I have not been to it. But he put new doors, locks, and an alarm system in it. He didn't want anybody taking his stolen stuff. Crooks don't like crooks."

"I should be able to find it in the county land records."

"No, it's not under his name. He uses a company name. It is something like ham hock, glam rock or something."

"Shamrock?"

"That's it. He thinks he's lucky Irish. Mostly he's a mean idiot."

"Anything else he's doing that might be dirty?"

"Not long ago, he started hauling out of Columbus. Real junk cars with no value. Made no sense to me. He brings them up here, then takes them over to the landfill for scrap. The scrap price doesn't even cover his towing cost. I think he is losing his mind. That and his meanness are why I left him again. Well, there's other stuff, but nothing to help you out. He gets to drinking and gets mean."

"I understand. I appreciate you telling me this."

"Don't tell Doyle you talked to me. But put him away if you can, so I can get my house back."

"I will do what I can. I can't promise what the police or judges will do."

"Won't be nothing if you go to that sheriff. They used to hate each other, but now they are best buddies."

"That is good to know. No, I won't be dealing with the sheriff. Do they have business together?"

"I don't know for sure. But he's over there for barbecue every month. And I think it was the sheriff that got him hauling out of Columbus since that other company lost the business. But I don't want trouble with the sheriff, either. I don't want to get between him and Doyle."

"Thanks again."

"You should call me, but after the divorce. Take me to dinner somewhere."

"I appreciate your help. I'll see what I can do with this information." She smiled and left with Alisha. She was attractive, if a little rough around the edges. But the thought of a date with Doyle's two-time ex-wife was unappealing. She seemed OK, so I hoped she would meet somebody good and get her house back once Doyle went away.

I put her information into my matrix, which was my brain until I could get home to my whiteboards. Doyle was running stolen parts besides his legitimate business. He and the sheriff were now buddies. And he was hauling worthless junk from Columbus to Hamilton County, maybe for the sheriff. I needed to look into that because it had to be something underhanded.

Based on Vicky's description, I located a likely structure on the county GIS property map. The owner was listed as Orchard Enterprises LLC. I cross-referenced that with the business records from the Secretary of State's business registration website. It was only three years old, so probably was not associated with the old orchard business. No officers were listed, but the registered agent was a lawyer in Hamilton County. Lawrence K. Endicott, IV. That was certainly an interesting coincidence. More digging and I found the property with the building prior to three years back was in an estate. I traced that name back to the original owner of the property, and the name was also the owner of the old orchard. I was betting Orchard Enterprises was Doyle's company, but he was using the name to deflect attention, so anyone searching would assume the property was still part of the old orchard business. Maybe Doyle was not dumb, or at least had a smart lawyer.

I found the deed, but the owner was listed as Shamrock, Inc. That matched what Vicky had told me, but was not definitive. I had one thing left to try. I looked up the county records of doing business as, or DBA for Shamrock, Inc. A Vicky Vickers was the signatory. I wondered if she even knew about it or whether Doyle and his lawyer listed her without her knowledge. Once this was over, I decided I would tell her. Maybe she could get something from Doyle she wasn't expecting.

CHAPTER TWENTY-FOUR

Millard came by the bookstore. He had already been to Mable's, so he brought a small bag for Kat. He was rapidly becoming one of her favorite humans. All I got was news.

"Hey James, I brought you some information. My day of the bet is rapidly approaching, and I need you to solve the case soon."

"I will do what I can. What do you have?"

"Doyle Vickers and the honorable Sheriff Jefferson Jackson are in business together."

"That confirms a rumor I just heard. Interesting, since I thought they were enemies."

"They were. Could not stand each other. The sheriff

even used a tow business in Columbus for county business to keep Doyle out."

"Columbus is a long way off."

"It is, but they had bought the sheriff to get the business. Then all of a sudden it stopped, and Doyle got the business. Then recently he gave the sheriff a car."

"A car? Wait, what kind of car?"

"An ugly loud green one. It's a Mustang."

"I've seen it, and it had no VIN, so it might be stolen."

"And then repainted a different color, if it was Mike's. Now go catch a murderer and make me some money."

"I'll see what I can do."

I called Lawrence K. Endicott's office since he was listed as the registered agent for Orchard Enterprises LLC. Once through the receptionist, I told him I had recently had a car towed by Doyle's company. By the time I got to my car, it had been stripped of wheels, sound system, and engine parts. I wanted to sue Doyle Vickers to recover the value of the property.

"I'm sorry, but I can't take the case," Larry told me. "It would be a conflict of interest, as I already represent Mr. Vickers."

"Thanks for your time. I will try somebody else."

It was not a sure thing, but there was the strong chance the link between Doyle and Larry the lawyer meant the Orchard Enterprises' property was Doyle's.

On a hunch I found a copy of some records I'd found in Joe Burrow's house after he died on my floor. Lawrence K. Endicott IV, was also the lawyer working with Joe and Benjamin Rawley from the Warm Springs campus. The people trying to run a major scam. Larry's name was coming up much too often for coincidence. Every sleazy criminal I knew in Hamilton County used him as a lawyer. I needed to give him a thorough vetting once the Vickers' case was finished.

Driving west, I found Doyle's secret shop. It was an older metal building sitting off of the highway. A cracked asphalt drive blocked by a simple but impressive metal gate flared out into a parking area in front of the building. A solid entry door was on the left and two bay doors on the right, all without windows. The grass was high everywhere, and the building had rust running down the sides from the roof. I don't know what it used to be, but now it was decrepit and ugly. A perfect place for Doyle to do something illegal. The property was surrounded by an old pecan orchard. The nut trees were past maturity and the whole orchard was covered in ten-year-old brush and young trees. Unsuitable to harvest pecans but great for deer and ticks.

I could park in front of the gate and walk around it, but it would be much too obvious. Vicky had already warned me the building had a security system. I assumed it included a camera or two. This was Bryan's operation if he could get a warrant. If not, maybe I'd come back and look around myself. I stopped to see Bryan on the way home.

"Bryan, I have a story for you. I talked to Vicky, Doyle's wife or former wife. She told me he runs a chop shop out near the interstate nobody knows about. I searched records and have some evidence it is true. Could be a place where Mike Vickers was murdered if Doyle was involved. Any way you can get a search warrant?"

"I can try, but I don't see how we can tie it to the

murder. If it is an illegal chop shop, then I should be able to start an investigation. I already know he's been taking totaled vehicles he picks up for towing and tacks them together for resale. He had somebody in another county forging the titles, changing them from salvage to clean. Illegal and unsafe, but profitable. But the shop is out of my jurisdiction. It would go to Sheriff Jackson instead."

"I was afraid of that. Also, I was told Doyle gave the sheriff the green Mustang. Is there a way to get a legal look at the car?"

"Only if we know for sure it is Mike's. If we get a warrant and it is not Mike's, it will alert the sheriff and probably ruin the case."

"Yeah, I was worried about that."

"Why did Vicky tell you about the shop? I guess she did not give you anything regarding Mike's murder."

"You are right, nothing on Mike. I think the chop shop was to get Doyle in trouble, even jailed. She wants him out of the way. But she also mentioned Doyle was hauling junk cars from Columbus to here. Some kind of deal with the sheriff. They are in business together."

"That is unexpected. But we can't bring in the sheriff."

"I thought so too. I don't have a plan to get us into the place and keep the sheriff out of it."

"I am afraid there is not a good way yet. If there was a clear business relationship, then I could tell the judge there was a conflict of interest, but he would probably still let the sheriff know."

"The same outcome if you go to the state police, the GBI?"

"Probably."

"I'll have to think about it. I would like to come up with a way to get inside and look around."

"I understand, but you know you can't. Even if you went in on your own and found something, it could taint any evidence enough to prevent its use in court."

"Understood, unfortunately. I won't be going out there until I can do it legally. Maybe I can goad Doyle into doing or saying something incriminating."

"Not your best use of time. I doubt he would give you anything about the shop, and he would likely hit you with a tire iron instead."

"Bryan, wouldn't Doyle have to tow cars from his chop shop to his legitimate business in Manchester right through Warm Springs?"

"I believe he would."

"Any chance his vehicle might be out of compliance and deserving of a traffic stop?"

"It could. But it would be a onetime thing. Can't legally keep stopping him without getting a harassment complaint. After the first stop, he would not have anything we need to find. He's smart enough to know the game. We would need to make the first stop count. As in finding drugs, a murder weapon, or a stolen Rembrandt."

"Once again, I don't know how to make that happen. I don't think he would know if he even had a Rembrandt."

"It is a quandary. If he is bringing one of the chopped vehicles to Manchester, there likely won't be anything in it anyhow. If he is bringing a junker from Columbus, there might be something if he's hauling pot for the sheriff. But I think he'd come up from the south to Manchester directly without coming through Warm Springs."

Near dark, I went on a walk around the outer loop. Millard saw me and waved me up to the house. This evening he was wearing a light grey vest, nothing flashy.

"Got your villain cornered yet?" he asked.

"Not yet, but getting closer."

"Good. Now I have some further news for you. Come in for a minute."

"Sure." I had no idea where Millard was going with the conversation.

"James, you see that room full of books? Look closer. See that section of geology books? That is what I studied in college."

"I thought you were interested in medicine."

"I was. That is why over half the books in here are about medicine. That is what I wanted to do, but I could not get into medical school. At least not the one I wanted. Geology was my second choice, which I studied at Leiden. I'm a big rock hound."

"I had no idea. I don't see any rock collections in here."

"They are all in the basement. Easier to go downstairs than upstairs. I didn't want all my specimens on this floor since there are so many. Just collect dust and strain the floor joists."

"That must be some collection."

"It is. I spent some years with two different companies traveling the world looking for ore deposits. Collected everything I could."

"Then what happened?"

"Got tired of it and came home. Got a job here on campus and moved up since the old guard was rapidly retiring and dying off. Took on the mayor role too.

Anyway, I know something about mining. I checked the Vickers property, and it was once a bauxite mine. Shipped out more than 400 tons right around WWI. Shut down after that as I guess they didn't need as much aluminum anymore. The last published ore report was in 1965. Lots of ore still in the ground."

"I took a quick look at that 1965 survey as well a few days ago, when researching Mike Vickers. But based on the current prices for bauxite and the metals in it, I don't see how mining it would be profitable."

"Since 1965, a few minerals they didn't assay have become more important. Rare minerals, especially earth elements. Bauxite tends to have some. Aluminum companies that mine and process it make a lot of profit from those secondary elements."

"What minerals and metals?"

"Things like gallium which is five hundred dollars a pound wholesale. Lately, it has been closer to eight hundred dollars a pound. Most bauxite has fairly low concentrations of gallium. My bet is the deposit here got tested and has high content. Other earth elements might also be present. Scandium is running about 2500 dollars a pound."

"Gallium is used in the computer industry, isn't it? And some of those things are used for high-tech batteries."

"Definitely."

"Something a computer guru from Silicon Valley would probably know."

"I think he would. Mike Vickers' land might be worth a whole lot of money. Although the real value is dependent on whether new technology gets developed to extract those elements, as current technology is inefficient and expensive. But for all I know, the technology might already be in development since there is a worldwide push for it."

"If Mike was tortured into signing away the rights, then maybe he was killed to make it look as if a rival pot importer did it. Then the computer guru escapes attention and gets away, if he's in league with Doyle. At the same time, Kapp puts a dent in one competitor, and the other is scrutinized for the killing, possibly putting it out of business. An all-around win for him."

"Yep, assuming the guy is that smart. And vicious."

"Maybe he's not, but he could have hired others to do the dirty work."

"True, but how are you going to prove it?"

"I don't know yet. But since Doyle just got the land back, I need to find who owns the mineral rights. Maybe Kapp and Doyle were in this together."

CHAPTER TWENTY-FIVE

I decided I needed a break and some time to myself. All the clutter in my brain trying to pull in every bit of information I could on the sheriff, Doyle, and Kapp had finally driven me temporarily mad. I turned off my phone and drove up on Pine Mountain to hike the trail. It was a wonderful two hours of walking without interruption, other than my brain going over iterations of information I already knew. Every few minutes, I made a conscious effort to shut it all down. It worked for about fifteen minutes, then the cycle began again. But overall, it was peaceful.

Once back at the car, I went home and began work on the cottage. I had decided to take out the ceiling. The bedroom area had a pine plank ceiling at nine feet that I would leave alone. The living area had an eight-foot ceiling made of sheetrock. I needed to remove all of it and hoped to find pine plank a foot above, like the bedroom. If it had been removed, then I might open the ceiling all the way up to the rafters. Then add spray foam insulation and cover with pine planks. That would give me a ceiling height of nearly fourteen feet in that section, and, depending on the construction, a low loft over the bedroom area.

It sounded so simple. Knock out a little sheetrock and let it fall down. But pulling down the ceiling meant the old sheetrock came down on me, along with decades of dust, pest poop from birds, bats, termites, and probably four different species of rodents. On my head and in my face. Even wearing a hat, protective glasses and a mask did not prevent everything from getting in my eyes, ears, nose, and mouth. If it had not been such a small area, less than two hundred square feet, I would have hired someone else to do it. But it did keep me from thinking about Mike Vickers and the several suspects.

I wondered if a bottle was going to fall down and hit me on the head. Unlikely, but anything could happen in the old cottage. That sent me down a tangential line of thinking about the old letter. I really needed to get up to the Georgia Archives and start thinking about a trip to New York to visit the other archive. Now that brought up an interesting idea; I could ask Donna if she wanted to go with me to New York. The Hudson Valley was a nice and scenic place. A bed-and-breakfast in a small town, located on or near a rail station. We could get an easy rail commute into New York City without driving if we wanted to see the sights or a Broadway show.

The letter was still in my thoughts, but I never seemed to get around to spending the days or weeks needed at the Georgia Archives to do research. Possibly because I knew the lengthy research might not even produce any tangible results. Or maybe the ghosts from the people in the letter were resisting my efforts. But I was betting on the former.

Two parts of the letter concerned me beyond the initial shock of the original two murders. First issue was the location of the body of the murdered fiancé. As best I could, I had laid out the directions in the letter. It was almost certainly buried on the edge of the golf course. Until I went there with a 300-foot tape measure, I would not be sure, but it was a safe bet it was in that location. What bothered me was that there was a slight chance it could be under the campus garden. But the odds of that were extremely small.

The other issue was the letter referenced a third murder. A person that had been on campus and possibly involved in the double murder was killed in another state. It was never solved, but could be related to the events on campus. I would need more research to determine that one.

I did not get further on my thought because I heard sirens crank up beside my house as tires spun, throwing gravel in the lot out front. Then the tires were squealing on the pavement as the car made the first turn on the asphalt. In my time on the RWS campus, I had never known the police to react like that. I went outside and also heard a distant siren on the main road at the bottom of the hill. I listened as the distant one went quiet a minute later. The new ones begun next door were going the same direction as the first one on the main road. A moment later, they were quiet. Whatever was happening was not far away.

I thought about driving over, but decided against it as I didn't need to add to a crowd that would soon gather, or clog traffic as whatever was happening was resolved. I heard more sirens begin wailing from the nearby hospital. From the sound, they went to the same point as the police cars, then went silent. Multiple police cars and two ambulances were a big deal in Warm Springs. There was no storm siren going off, so my worst fear, a train derailment in town, had likely not happened. A derailment itself wasn't too worrying, but the chemical cargo from the train cars and tankers always worried me.

I went back inside as I figured someone would tell me tomorrow at the store or Mable's what had happened. Kat rubbed my leg, then clawed the nearest chair as a signal to let her out. She was frisky and ready to chase the chipmunks in the yard. I went upstairs to write since I had been neglecting that part of my professional life. Actually, it was the only part of my life that was professional, and I liked it that way.

Two hours later, someone was knocking on my front door. I pocketed my little 9mm friend I had been carrying lately and went downstairs. Through the glass door I saw a haggard-looking Bryan waiting on the porch. I thought of something witty to greet him with, but thought it was inappropriate based on his tired look.

"Evening James."

"Hi Bryan. You are not looking too fresh at the moment."

"It has been a long, bad day in some ways. But maybe good will come from it."

"What's wrong?"

"My deputies were approaching the city limits and about to turn around. They saw Doyle Vickers towing a car into town just as a sheriff's car pulled him over. Doyle jumped out and began yelling at the sheriff's car. The county deputies got out and pulled their guns. Doyle reached into his truck and brought out a gun."

"I'm guessing it did not go well."

"No, it did not. There was some more yelling, then Doyle started shooting. The sheriff's deputies returned fire and hit Doyle several times. My guys were right there when one of the county deputies went up to Doyle and was about to shoot him in the head. There was a tense moment, but he did not shoot Doyle."

"Did Doyle make it?"

"He was alive when they put him in the ambulance. I just got word that he died."

"Any idea why he went berserk?"

"We are going through his truck and the junk car but so far have not found anything. Maybe he was just stupid and mean."

"I feel bad for your deputies being put in that position, but I don't feel a great sense of loss at Doyle's passing."

"I'd say the whole town feels that way."

"I do wonder what the sheriff's deputies were doing in town."

"They said they thought the tow was unsafe."

"Do you believe that?"

"No, I don't. I think Doyle was going to get shot whether he pulled a gun first or not."

"Does this mean that Doyle's building over by the interstate is now in play for you to open up and investigate?"

"It is since he was killed in town, and that is why I am here. The search warrant will be ready in the morning and I'd like you to come with us. I imagine whatever is out there it will have some bearing on either the Vickers case or the pot operation."

"I'd love too. My prediction is a few more pieces of the puzzle will fall together."

"I hope so. We need a few breaks to get the sheriff put away. Come over at nine in the morning."

"Will do. Take care and goodnight."

Doyle's outburst was an interesting development. There was no good reason for him to do what he did, unless he suspected the sheriff's deputies were going to do him harm. But it opened up his secret garage for a search. My instincts told me we would find evidence linking him to Mike's murder, pot smuggling, or both. But I had been wrong before.

I rode with Bryan to Doyle's secret garage. The gate had already been opened by an enterprising deputy with a portable grinder. I could still smell the hot metal as we passed by. Two cars were already parked in front of the building. One was from Bryan's department, and the other was unmarked, but I knew it was from the state. The Georgia Bureau of Investigation was on the scene, which meant two of my biggest non-fans were here. Woods and Sims still hated me from previous encounters. I was not sure whether I'd get ignored or plastered with snark.

We got out of the car and Woods and Sims completely ignored me. My prayers were answered, but I prepared a snappy riposte for later. We waited as two more cars pulled in from Bryan's department.

"OK people, we are going to remove the lock from the front door and move into the building," Bryan said. "I'd like everyone to wear the disposable shoe covers along with the regular gloves today. After we go through the building, we will meet back here, then make two passes around the exterior of the building. Any questions?"

"Nobody from the sheriff's office is coming?" I asked.

"They were not invited. Let's go in." A bolt cutter made short work of the large padlock on the front door. We went in and someone found the lights. Luckily Doyle had paid the electric bill, so we didn't have to wander around with flashlights. We spread out and walked around a disorganized area full of large car parts strewn around. Metal shelves scattered around had more organization and held smaller, more expensive car parts. Overall, it looked better than Doyle's official garage in Manchester, but not by much. Not knowing exactly where to go, I followed Bryan as he moved around the building.

I heard someone call out and we all moved toward the back, left corner. Behind some tall cabinets set up to form a "room" a tarp was spread out. One chair was on the tarp and two others were a few feet away and facing the single chair. The single chair was a black upholstered office chair, an older model with metal arms and frame, unlike the cheap plastic models. The seat of the chair had a single hole in it and the black fabric was splotchy white. A stink of chlorine lay heavy in the air.

"Watch out, there is a strong chlorine smell under the tarp," someone said.

"I believe this is now an official crime scene," GBI agent Woods said.

I could not resist goading the man. "Or it could be where Mike Vickers met a tragic but accidental death," I said.

He glowered at me. Sims, the attractive female GBI agent, did the same. They had closed Tammy Wilkins' murder as an accident before I proved them wrong. It was immature of me, but it felt good.

CHAPTER TWENTY-SIX

"James, can you come over to my office?" Bryan asked on the phone.

"Sure, I'll be right there," I replied.

It had been three days since Doyle's death and two days since we had visited his secret shop. A minute later I was at Bryan's door since I had not left to open the bookstore. The opening would be late today. Bryan got up and closed the door. Uh oh, this was going to be good.

"I received a package in the mail yesterday," Bryan said. "It is from Doyle Vickers. Posthumously, of course."

"I assume it was not a bomb."

"In a way, that is exactly what it is. I read the contents

last night, several times. I made a copy this morning and would like you to read it and give me your assessment."

"That may take a while."

"Not really. It is fairly short and specific. You will get slowed up because Doyle's horrible penmanship is only exceeded by his lack of grammar." Bryan handed me a document. I began reading or trying to.

"You were not kidding. Based on the level of writing skill, I feel this would be better written in crayon."

"The content more than makes up for the presentation, fortunately."

It was quiet as I spent the next ten minutes deciphering the papers. Doyle had gone off on a few tangents and rants full of misspelled curse words. But the summary of the document was a precise detail of Sheriff Jefferson Jackson's recent activities of importing, transporting, and distributing marijuana. Dates and amounts that Doyle transported from boats on the river south of Columbus to several points in Hamilton County where containers or old homesites were located. A list of people meeting and paying him, mostly deputies and the sheriff. It ended with a sentence predicting the sheriff was setting him up for murder and drug dealing, and this would be sent in case he was killed by the police. I assume he meant the sheriff or his deputies. There was no confession of the murder of Mike Vickers, any mention of his recent land acquisition, or Kapp Hendriks.

"If any of this is true, the sheriff is in trouble," I said.

"I sent this to the GBI this morning. By fax, since it is the only official method recognized by state or federal agencies."

"Yeah, I don't understand how a fax that can be read by anybody in the office is a secure communication. He was afraid the sheriff was setting him up to be killed."

"Seems he was right. And it explains something found last night. A bag of cocaine was in the junk car, in the gas tank."

"The sheriff?"

"Yeah, no question. The bag still had the ID tag from the county sheriff's office evidence locker inside it. They really did plan to frame Doyle. They didn't expect my people to be there to keep the planted drugs from being recovered by them. If they had stopped him a hundred yards sooner, it would have been county jurisdiction and they would have gotten away with it."

"Can the sheriff be tied directly to the pot smuggling other than Doyle's letter?"

"Search teams are on the way to check the boats as we speak at the marina down south. Those and the cocaine bag are enough to start a serious investigation. But here is the real prize." Bryan put a cassette player on his desk and hit play. The voices were muted, but I made out Doyle's, the sheriff's, and a third unknown voice. It was made at what must have been a pot drop off when Doyle got paid. I heard specific directions about where to put the pot, the amount of it, and a potential dollar value. And the sheriff thanking Doyle for the green Mustang. "The tape and a ledger of all the pot runs Doyle made for the sheriff were also in the package. A couple of the runs Doyle made were taking cash back to a boat. Doyle wrote that he overheard someone on the boat say they were about to start a multi-day trip to Belize."

"Isn't that one of the countries with laws favoring secret offshore accounts?"

"It certainly is."

"That package might make the difference," I said.

"As soon as the boats are in custody, a search warrant will be issued for the sheriff's property, including his office and vehicles. One of the boats was supposed to be arriving last night, so with Doyle dead it might not have been unloaded and the pot transported yet. All in all, I think we have him."

"And you already know what to search for on his property."

"Yep, looks like we will be digging to find those septic tanks."

"The only thing we don't have is Mike's murderer."

"Once this comes out and the rats scatter, somebody might talk."

"I hope so. I think Doyle did it, but I expect he got help from the sheriff, at least in detaining Mike."

I left Bryan's office feeling better. The threat from the sheriff should soon be over. The feeling did not last long. I received a call from Atlanta that I needed to return on a burner phone. The past days I had resisted the urge to call them for help on the Mike Vickers' case. I had used their help on the Tammy Wilkins murder and wanted to limit my contact with the Dixie Mafia as much as possible. But I had to call them back.

"Hey kid. We appreciated the property deeds. That was a nice gesture. Made us whole on the Joe Burrows deal."

"Well, I killed the guy that owed you money. It was more of a self-preservation move."

"Still, it is something we won't forget. You chose not to go in with us, but you still show respect. Because of that, we wanted to give you a warning. Some people are not happy about you down there and might cause trouble."

"Oh, the guys from New Orleans. I imagine they are not happy since he owed them a lot of money, too."

"Actually, no, they are not the problem. When they found out he was two-timing his gambling debt, they took out a million-dollar life insurance policy. When you killed him, they doubled their money. But they did not get their payoff from the condo scam. They aren't friends, but neither are they enemies."

"OK, that is good to know. But who might be after me then?"

"Local guys. The dummy you took out last year was cutting side deals with all kinds of people in the area. Guys running schemes with timber cutting, concrete work, demolition teams, politicians, everybody planning to make money from the big thing down there. Then recently you got some new enemies. People down there protecting their illegitimate business interests."

"That doesn't narrow it down much. Could be half the county."

"Yeah, our information is not real specific. Just watch out down there."

"Is there a contract out on me yet?"

"No, not yet. Some questions were asked, but no money was put down. May not happen."

"Would you guys take the contract?"

"Probably. Then we'd tell you, so you could leave town

or get ready. After that, we'd drop it and somebody else would pick it up. Give you at least a couple of weeks."

"Thanks for the heads up."

"No problem. If you need help with any of that, you know how to find us."

That was interesting. My life went from quiet and peaceful to potentially having a contract placed to kill me. I really was making friends.

Two days later, I saw Bryan at the cafeteria. He had a darker suntan than usual but looked tired.

"Bryan, you look like you need to be in the office more."

"Never thought I'd say it, but I agree. I've been walking all over the sheriff's property."

"How is it going?"

"We found two septic tanks out there. Both were well hidden, and we might have missed them if we had not known they were there."

"So once the property is seized and put up for sale at auction, there will be a rush to put in bids. I'm sure the rumor of a third tank is in the gossip chain."

"It may be sold for more than it's worth. In fact, I bet it goes for at least twice the tax value, considering what was in the two tanks we found."

"What was in them?"

"Each had more than five million dollars, a few guns, a bugout bag, and one had a few hundred pounds of pot vacuum-packed in several bricks."

"The prospect of another five million in the ground out there is going to drive people crazy."

"I already had the county put a watch on the property.

Although since half the deputies are in custody, these guys are coming in from neighboring counties for extra shifts. We checked the places Doyle listed as delivery sites, but there was not a tank there either."

"It will be a myth soon, the lost treasure of Hamilton County. Bring a shovel and metal detector, vacation in Warm Springs. Somebody could set up a concession and charge diggers five dollars a day. It would be similar to the diamond mine in Arkansas."

"It may come to that. We could offer a finder's fee if they run across it. But I'm pretty sure it is not there."

"Has the sheriff admitted anything now that he's in custody?"

"Not really. He is walking a fine line between defending against Doyle's accusations and incriminating himself. He said Doyle was trying to frame him for several things, including Mike's murder. Claims Doyle was mad about the high contributions to the sheriff's charity required to keep the county towing business. Doyle had run out of money and gave him a car for the latest payment."

"That sounds lame. Can he sell that?"

"I don't think the District Attorney buys it at all. Not with all the evidence that is building up. I don't think we need to worry about the sheriff for at least twenty years."

"I think Doyle was going to turn him in eventually. He had dealings with Kapp Hendriks, so that would get rid of some competition."

"Makes sense, but not relevant now. Could have also been personal. I heard the sheriff was visiting Vicky Vickers in his spare time."

"That was a whole new level of stupid on his part. Or maybe Vicky is better at the game than I thought. With Doyle dead, I bet she gets everything."

There was at least one major loose end in the Mike Vickers case I wanted to check on. I drove south the evening after talking to Bryan to see my new acquaintance. I heard Kapp Hendriks was leaving Hamilton County, and I wanted to talk to him before he left. When I drove up, he was outside his house, a mid-century modern outside of Hamilton.

"Hi Kapp."

"Hello Dr. Wilder. I'm not too surprised to see you here."

"I wanted to say goodbye. I thought it an odd coinci-dence that you were leaving so soon after Doyle and the sheriff went down. But then I realized you must have made that decision some time ago to have already sold your farms."

"True, I was leaving anyway. Doyle was an inflamed boil, likely to explode at any time. I thought the sheriff would neutralize him since they had business together and he likely thought the same about Doyle. It was no surprise that it happened the way it did. But things were too volatile for me here. And honestly, I'm not cut out to live in the Georgia countryside. I'll do better back on the West Coast."

"Seems appropriate for your background."

"Perhaps you are here for more than a goodbye. I know you have been investigating the death of Mr. Mike Vickers."

"True, I have been. A consultant to the Warm Springs Campus Police."

"I never thought you were a journalist. Strange that the Warm Springs police got the Vickers' case."

"It was all about jurisdiction. The body dumpers got stupid and left it on the wrong side of the boundary. Same thing happened with Doyle's shooting."

"Interesting how such minor details changed the entire outcome. A few more feet and the sheriff would have gotten both cases. Little or nothing would have come from it, rather than the extensive changes now occurring."

"Fate is fickle, but Doyle's package changed everything, anyway. I wanted it to implicate you as well. But technically, you've done nothing that can be proven illegal. You might have goaded Doyle, but he likely would have done what he did anyway. Maybe you even prodded the sheriff."

"James, I did not goad them. In fact, your actions resulting in their demise have unloaded a burden."

"How's that?"

"The sheriff was extorting me for protection."

"So, he didn't arrest you as long as you paid him."

"Exactly. Now I don't have to do that."

"But had you stayed you'd have to pay the next sheriff or risk getting found out."

"This episode made me realize I was in the wrong place at the wrong time. All my growing activities have ceased, and all evidence has been expunged."

"I guess you'll have to rely on your legitimate business interests."

"Not really. The produce did little more than break even, once freight was included to get it to market. The boutique pot market was what bankrolled everything."

"What do you do now?"

"I've sold what I can. I'm moving back west, where I can grow legally. Now that I have proven my marketing concept, I can do it legally and still make money."

"What about the Vickers' mineral interest? I assume you put that concept into Doyle's head."

"I may have mentioned it to Doyle, even exaggerated its worth. But that was never a legitimate concept. Doyle became convinced he was sitting on millions and wanted a partner, at least so he said. But once I invested any money, I knew he would betray me and turn me in for marijuana growing. He even put that in the mineral rights contract. Some clause about our partnership being dissolved if one party was found to be involved in illicit activities. That tipped me off."

"He wanted your money and then would put you away, keep the supposed millions from the mine for himself."

"That was his plan. But the only way to realize any of that was through technology yet to be invented. He did not own enough property encompassing the bauxite reef for mining to be profitable. With the current methods, even extracting the entire known reef would not have yielded much profit."

"But his illicit activities broke the mineral rights agreement, anyway."

"That was ironic. Not that Doyle knew the nuance. Maybe someday the land could be worth millions. But it is just as likely new elements or different ways to make semi-conductors will be invented, and the land goes back to being worth only what someone will pay to farm it or grow timber."

"But your interest probably pushed Doyle into killing Mike."

"I seriously doubt it. Doyle had already decided to do it, and the sheriff was a half-step behind. According to Doyle, the sheriff thought Mike was going to turn him in once they refused to hire him. For all I know, they did it together."

"But with Mike and his gang gone, it also eliminated a potential competitor."

"Perhaps. That is the nature of the business. But too late for me to consider staying."

"Well, I would wish you luck, but I figure you can buy your way in to your next venture."

"Obviously." Kapp's phone rang. "This is Kapp." He listened for a moment. "What?" he yelled. "Everything is gone?" Kapp uttered a few curse words and hung up the phone.

"Bad news?"

"Did you do this?"

"Uh, did I do what? I'm very sure I have done nothing pertaining to whatever you are cursing at."

"Someone has set my grow houses on fire. They were mostly empty, and I had canceled the insurance. But my trucks were burned as well. The ones already loaded with the genetic stock for the marijuana I needed for my new venture."

"Nope, not me or mine."

"I didn't think it was you since you have nothing to gain. But someone is targeting me. I don't think any of Doyle's family knows or cares. The sheriff and his people are incarcerated. At least the ones I know about."

"The sheriff still has a lot of friends in the county. Even I have been warned about them. Sorry about your loss. I'm sure you can get started with new weed stock."

"I have no choice. But yes, although I've lost a lot of money, I'll recover soon enough."

"Goodbye Kapp."

"So long, Dr. Wilder."

I left Kapp's place feeling like justice had not been done. But that was soon rectified. My phone rang on the way home. "Hello," I answered. The other end of the connection was on speaker.

"Thanks for the tip, felt like we were back in the sand," said a male voice.

"Yeah, this was a lot of fun," said a second female voice.

"I'm glad you had a good time. I'm not sure how complicit Kapp was in Mike's death, but he had some accountability coming."

"He got it. Thanks again for letting us know about Kapp. We got to have our fun in Mike's memory."

"Glad I could help. Bye."

Mike's overseas military buddies had put their skills to use. Kapp really did have it coming. I'm sure he implied to Doyle that Mike was standing between him and a fortune, and I'm sure he let the sheriff know Mike was a threat. Regardless of whether that was the tipping point that got Mike killed, Kapp was potentially going to see a profit from his dealings in Hamilton County. Now he was not. And Mike's friends got a little payback for Kapp's part in his death.

The next day, the news would report a series of recent fires in the south part of the county. Several former chicken houses converted to hydro- and aquaponics had burned, with loss of all contents. Nearby trucks had also been destroyed. Kapp really was out of business in Hamilton County. Nobody mentioned the pungent smell emanating from the burning trucks.

I drove back to Warm Springs, pleased with how things had worked out with Kapp and Mike's buddies. My main regret so far was not proving without a doubt whether Doyle or the sheriff had killed Mike. Doyle was still the best bet since there was a probable kill site at his secret warehouse. Still, I just wanted a solid confirmation or confession to seal it. I also thought how my sleuthing might have had some influence, but the bad guys going after each other was what really broke everything open.

I passed the entrance to the campus and found myself turning right in Warm Springs to go up Pine Mountain. Past the Little White House and the "Deer Crossing" sign, then I pulled off the road to the right. Inside the trees where Mike's body was found, I found nothing. No sign he had ever been there, no ghost, not even police tape. There was probably a metaphor for how I felt, but I was not in the mood. I left and turned the car around to go home.

From this angle there was a glint from the bottom of the Deer Crossing sign. A black box was attached to the signpost and looked like one of the boxes that counted traffic. But there was no cable across the road. On a hunch, I pulled over and went back to look at the box. The glint came from round glass embedded in the box that looked suspiciously like a camera lens. I looked over the box but found no markings other than a Georgia Fish and Wildlife Department sticker. I had gone by the sign at least 50 times and never noticed the box before.

When home, I called the GF&W number to ask about the box. Not surprisingly, it took multiple transfers and three separate calls to find the person I needed to talk to. It was almost as if the system was designed to foil most phone calls. But I knew the system and how to be persistent. I asked about the box and found it was a camera system, including infrared, set to count the number of times deer crossed the road, along with vehicle traffic. The camera was triggered by movement. It was a trial program designed to collect data on deer and vehicle interactions at night, in an effort to find a strategy to minimize collisions. I asked if vehicles triggered the camera and got an affirmative answer. But only vehicles at night, and due to the volume, data from the images were compiled, and the images deleted monthly.

I told the researcher I was consulting for the Warm

Springs police and a murder was committed nearby, or at least a body dumped near the Pine Mountain box. She understood and asked me to have Bryan request the month's images either in writing or via email. I readily agreed and went to tell Bryan the good news. Or maybe good news, depending on what images were visible the night Mike Vickers' body was dumped.

Later, I sat in Bryan's office to view the video feed sent over from GF&W for the night we needed. The video images played from approximately two hours before and two hours after the coroner said the body had likely been dumped in the woods. We could widen the range depending on what we found after the initial search.

The feed was boring enough that we fast-forwarded it. Then Bryan hit the stop button. "That is Doyle's truck," he said.

It was a Southern cliché, a large pickup jacked up at least 12 inches, with oversized tires and wheel spacers, so they stuck out either side of the truck. Negating any effect of the wheel wells and mud flaps. An asinine thing to do, as the side of the truck was always dirty and over time, the paint was peppered with rock hits. It also had the towing mirrors that stuck out two feet from either side of the truck. A pathetic cry of someone trying to claim manhood by taking up more lane space than other males. It also had a magnetic sign that said "Vickers Towing" on the side. Bryan backed up the video and slowed the speed as we watched it go past the camera. We waited and saw it return.

"It goes up Pine Mountain past the Little White House, then comes back down less than ten minutes later," Bryan said. "Would you say that gave him enough time to pull over, carry the body into the woods, turn around and come back?"

"I'd say that. And Doyle was big enough to carry the body by himself."

"That should do it. We have enough evidence to impound the truck for testing. If Mike Vickers' DNA shows up, then I'm good at calling it a murder committed by Doyle Vickers and closing the case."

CHAPTER TWENTY-EIGHT

I drove south toward Shiloh and the other side of Pine Mountain. I missed a couple of turns, but eventually found my destination. Turning onto the old road in the woods, I found the brush was still thick and the low hanging pine branches made me cringe as they scraped along my car's paint. Having a four-wheel-drive vehicle came in handy on a trip like this.

The clearing was as I remembered it. Some of the weeds were crushed, as I had noticed on the road on the drive in. Off to the edge, there was a fresh mound of red clay piled against the woods. I walked around the clearing, then over to the abandoned cargo container. It looked and smelled as before, which meant stinky, dank, and covered with graffiti. The only thing new was a poorly spray-painted circle on the floor. Outside, I scrambled up the back above one side of the container and saw the dirt that partially buried it was newly disturbed on both sides and the back.

Based on observational data, the container had been picked up and moved, or more likely propped up, and something buried underneath it. I removed a portable battery-powered grinder and saw from my car, along with extra batteries just in case. I donned personal protective equipment and went into the container to remove the floor where the circle was painted. The thick plywood cut easily enough, and I had to cut two metal floor beams once the wood was gone. Below me was a black plastic cap approximately two feet in diameter, marking a buried septic tank underneath.

An hour later, I had five million dollars in cash in the car, along with a bag containing blank passports, driver's licenses, credit cards, and a key to a safe deposit box. No pictures on the documents and none of the names were anyone I knew. I had taken several guns out of the tank as well, then made them inoperable with the grinder. Those were now scattered in the woods. There was a large duffel bag of shrink-wrapped pot, most of which was now scattered on the ground along the road. One large brick was with me.

Once home, I unloaded the money in my basement. My new project was going to be getting rid of five million as quickly as possible without getting caught. My initial thought was anonymously gifting a duffel bag of 500,000 dollars to each of ten charities in the area. Keeping the money was a terrible idea that would get me into trouble, killed, or both.

Sheriff Jefferson Jackson was smart to keep his illegal assets close and buried on his property. It was easier to control and oversee. But he was smart to diversify the assets and put some of them elsewhere in case he was on the run or got caught. Even if he had to spend twenty years in prison, he would be set up if he still had five million in ready cash waiting upon release. This was at least one of his failsafe caches. I was sure there was at least one more, but I had no leads or intention to find it. My reason to take the one I found was to keep the sheriff from profiting. It could have gone to the police, but eventually the government would have gotten it and probably bought more armored SUVs and automatic weapons for the police department.

I went to several stores and thrift shops and paid cash for ten duffels. I put equal bundles of bills into each bag until the pile of money was gone, except for one bag, which was $100,000 short. They were all stacked in the basement. I didn't bother locking the door when I left.

Donna and I arrived at Millard's house the next evening. We had been invited to one of his card game nights. At least, that is what he told me. But it was not what I had expected. I pictured a bunch of grizzled old men playing poker, drinking whiskey and smoking cigars. Instead, it was several couples drinking Aperol spritzes or iced tea with fresh flowers decorating the room. It was more of a party and no card game.

Bryan was there with Trish, Lottie, George and his wife, and the surprise of the night—Alisha and Robert. Plus, Ison and Beverly, and several older gentlemen I did not know. I think they were part of Millard's group of card sharks and octogenarian sleuth researchers.

Lottie was wearing a stylish red evening gown with white flowers in her hair, diamond earrings, and necklace. She looked the grande dame part. Millard was dressed in a white shirt with a bright scarlet waistcoat and black pants. Topped off with a black bowtie and black and white shoes. The two of them together looked like a pair from a 1940s movie. Donna wanted to meet everyone, so we did. Robert and Alisha were last.

"Hi Alisha. This is Donna Childers."

"Hi Donna, I'm Alisha, and this is Robert."

The two women began talking as Robert and I walked to get a drink for us and them. It was a good time for a brief chat.

"Hi Robert," I said. "I think it was time we were properly introduced. I'm James Wilder."

"I know. At some point, I thought we would meet. I wanted to thank you for what you did to Joe Burrows. But more importantly, for being nice to Alisha. It meant a lot to her."

"You are welcome on both counts. Alisha is a great person. We've really enjoyed having her volunteer in the garden. I guess you know your daughter has been adopted as our mascot."

"Yeah, Alisha told me all about it."

"I know you are not on campus, but if you ever want to work with Alisha in the garden, we'd be happy to have you."

"Thanks, maybe sometime. Between the business, my boys and our little one, I hardly seem to have any time."

"I imagine you are quite busy. The offer stands. And feel free to join us for any of our monthly picnics."

"Thank you."

I mingled in the crowd as best I could. I wasn't good at mingling and the crowd was small. Millard and Lottie did a ballroom dance in the large central hall slash living space. They obviously knew how to dance. Millard was taking some gummies I had given him for his hip. Donna asked if I wanted to try dancing, but I declined. I told her it was for the best, as otherwise she would know how it felt to be trampled by a buffalo. But we agreed to look into dance lessons. I would be fine with dancing if I knew how.

"Hey, did you hear about the lawyer from Hamilton getting arrested this week?" Millard asked me later. "I think his name was Endicott. Apparently, he was involved in the sheriff's drug business."

"No I had not heard. How did the police find him?"

"He was not a smart person to be a lawyer. They found a ten-pound brick of marijuana and $100,000 cash in his car after a tip."

"Yeah, I guess that wasn't smart."

"He was looking at possession and intent to distribute. But now he has decided to give testimony to the grand jury and is looking at probation. He was representing some really bad people by setting up shell companies and LLCs. He gave them all up, and now the state and federal police have about three years of work to unravel those businesses and the crooks behind them. Apparently, the whole region was using him to set up bogus corporations."

"I guess he will lose his law license if nothing else. He can't give up his clients without some repercussions."

"Maybe, but he thinks one of his clients framed him, so he is taking them all down. Not everybody realizes yet how big this is. Could be the biggest reckoning for criminals in middle Georgia in the last 50 years, according to our group."

"That sounds good. I'm glad to hear it can get cleaned up." Most people on the periphery of the conversation were nodding and agreeing with everything, but two, Lottie and Bryan, were watching me like a hawk. "Maybe you should come up with a name for your group. Octodetectives or something."

"We might, but it won't be that. You must be terrible at marketing."

"So I've heard. Did anyone get the betting pool?"

"Lottie did. She bet on you, but put some extra money on the outer limit. She figured you would get the murderer, but it would take longer, and she was right."

I took Donna home later since we were being idiots and behaving ourselves per our agreement. I got home and sat on the front porch since it was a nice evening. Shortly I heard footsteps. They were not unexpected.

"Good evening Bryan. How did you like the party?"

"Hey James. I thought it was nice. I'm glad to see Millard up and around."

"Me too. What can I do for you this fine evening?"

"Have you heard anything about a cargo container site being dug up?"

"Can't say that I have. Why?"

"The old pot shed, the container we visited a while

back, was vandalized. Somebody cut the floor out, and it seems the third septic tank had been buried underneath."

"Well now we know where it was. I suppose it was empty when you found it."

"It was. There were some pieces of guns out in the woods I assume were inside the tank, but nothing else was found."

"I guess the sheriff got robbed. It's a shame he will never see the money. Thinking about that, Bryan, maybe you can help me."

"What's that?"

"Got time to look at something? I need to get an idea about how to move some items in the basement."

"Sure, I can go now if it won't take long."

We walked around to the back of my house to the basement door. It was unlocked, as always. I turned on the light as we went in. A few bugs scurried out of the light.

"Bryan, I have these ten duffels down here. I need ideas on how to move them."

"You don't need me for that, James, just pick them up by the handles," he said sarcastically.

"Surprisingly, I had figured that out. More specifically, I need ideas on how to deliver them."

"OK, first, what is in them?"

"Five hundred thousand dollars each. Although one has only four hundred thousand dollars."

"You have got to be kidding, right?"

"Nope."

"You've really got five million dollars sitting here."

"Yep, for several days now. I liberated it from a septic

tank in the wild where there was no owner listed. Finders keepers, I guess, but I don't want it."

"And you are asking me about where to deliver it?"

"That's right, it's sitting here waiting to be delivered to ten different charities, anonymously. Very anonymously."

Bryan stood silently, working out the ramifications and jurisdictions that might be involved. Just like I had, but maybe he would come up with something I had not thought of.

"Nobody knows about this?"

"Just you, just now."

"You left no evidence?"

"None, especially no fingerprints or DNA."

"Where did you get the duffels?"

"Multiple stores and paid cash."

"Was there anything in the tank pointing to where it came from or who put it there?"

"Nothing I could find with a thorough search."

"Did you leave a trail when you went looking for it? Something that somebody else could trace?"

"Hardly. I went there on a hunch."

"Was there anything else in the tank?"

"Guns, which I destroyed. A large duffel of pot bricks, most of which I destroyed by opening and dumping it along the road. Except for one brick."

"Once again, you did not leave any evidence of your presence?"

"No, nothing. And by the way, you don't know there is even any money in these duffels other than me telling you there is. At this point, you are not involved. Walk away if you need to."

"The sheriff and his cronies will hear about the container and tank being found. They can't do anything about it without admitting more guilt. They will be mad but can't do much, especially if you were careful. From the law side, we have some evidence of a third septic tank being in the sheriff's possession, but only because you told me. With no official identifiers, I think you are in a grey area. If you don't keep and don't report it, there are no taxes, but if you did keep it, there could be tax evasion charges. You found money in the woods and are passing it on to charities anonymously. Let me think some more. OK, I still think a DA could bring a case against you if they knew, but I'm not sure of the outcome. What did you want me to do?"

"What you just did. Go through it and give me an opinion on how much trouble I could be in from the legal side. And since we've been talking, I think I have a delivery method. But I have one favor to ask."

"OK, but I have to ask first. You said you got rid of most of the pot except for one brick. And one of the bags is short $100,000 dollars. Where did that go?"

"I contributed it toward a good cause. In fact, I think both are probably back in your possession by now."

Bryan started laughing. I did too, since it had been a good evening.

EPILOGUE

The asinine lime green Mustang with racing harnesses instead of seat belts had been towed into the impound lot but not processed, so it was not locked up behind the gate. Bryan made sure of that. Anybody with keys could take it. Bryan had given me a spare key, so all I had to do was bring it back to the front of the lot. Where there were no cameras.

I took the car from where it was parked and drove through the evening, distributing duffel bags at various buildings around the area. I had previously checked all the locations and stayed away from places with obvious surveillance cameras. I'm sure I missed some. But charities rarely had to worry about strong security.

Anyway, since I was in Mike Vickers' car, stolen by Doyle Vickers after he killed Mike and given it to the crooked sheriff as a bribe, I didn't think they could trace it to me. Just in case, I wore a silly cowboy hat, just like General Custer. And I had on a fake Santa beard. It seemed appropriate for the circumstances. But now my sleigh ride was over. I had to get back home and make a chocolate cake with Donna.

The Roosevelt Warm Springs, or RWS campus exists mostly as described. A few liberties were taken with details. For example, there is an abandoned camp on site by the lake, but it was not a Boy Scout retreat.

Similarly, the town of Warm Springs is mostly as described. Unfortunately, Mable's Diner does not exist and to my knowledge never has. Other restaurants and stores are there, however.

A significant change I made was to create the fictitious Hamilton County. It was carved from the actual counties of Meriwether, Harris, Troup and Talbot. The new county includes the towns of Warm Springs, Manchester, Pine Mountain, Shiloh, Woodland, and Hamilton, plus most of the ridge of Pine Mountain, and all of Roosevelt State Park. It was done to simplify jurisdictions of the towns, state park and RWS campus. I made the county seat the town of Hamilton. It is a real county seat, but for Harris County.

The Roosevelt Warm Springs campus and the town of Warm Springs are worth a visit, as well as the Little White

House. All were amazing places in the time of Franklin D. Roosevelt, and hopefully the RWS campus will be again.

Kat does exist and will welcome visitors. Kat is not her real name—I've used a pen name for her to protect her true identity. But if you see a fluffy tabico miniature Maine Coon cat eyeing chipmunks in front of the house, you'll know it's her.

ABOUT THE AUTHOR

I'm D. Smith, a native Georgian that can't seem to stay in the state for long. Tried a number of states and Europe so far, and lately have settled in Asheville, North Carolina. But I do now have a house on the Warm Springs Roosevelt campus, so soon that will be home.

I've been a lot of things over my work career, but I've put that nonsense behind me. The travel in America, Europe, and Asia was useful as an author. And finally the Ph.D. came in useful—for writing about food.

I now write books and pet cats for fun, since neither pays very well. I'm weaning myself away from social media, but the links below give a little more background and perhaps foreground on the author known as D. Smith.

RECIPE

ROASTED PERSIMMONS

This is a recipe with an unusual star ingredient. Persimmons, specifically Asian persimmons. You can try American persimmons when they ripen in the fall, but the soft texture and small size makes them better suited to custard or ice cream. Of course, never serve them green unless you are experiencing unwanted guests.

The Ingredients
>2 firm, ripe Asian persimmons
>2 tablespoons turbinado (or brown) sugar
>1/2 cup mascarpone
>1 tablespoon spoon honey
>1/4 teaspoon cinnamon

The Process
Cut the persimmons in half along the equator. Cut out the brown center of the northern hemisphere. Turn over so the flat, cut section faced up. No need to peel persimmons.

Sprinkle the sugar on top. Add other spices of choice, but be careful. The persimmons have a distinct flavor, but it is subtle.

Put in a baking pan and cook at least 10 minutes at 375 F. This cooks the persimmons. Then turn on the broiler (usually 550 F) but keep watch to not burn the sugar on top. A nice brown bubbly caramel means they are done.

As the persimmons cool a few moments, stir the cinnamon into the honey, then stir that into the mascarpone. Add a large spoonful to each persimmon half and serve. Save the other half for breakfast.

Finishing Notes

This is a simple and tasty dessert. Persimmons evoke fall, but the sweetened and spiced mascarpone can pull this dish into the warm months as well. If you cannot find mascarpone, use whipped cream, or in an emergency, pull the tub of white stuff out of the freezer. Mascarpone or whipped cream can be more exciting when amaretto, vanilla, or mini chocolate chips are added.

If you want to go full fall, toss a few marshmallows onto the persimmon tops when you turn on the broiler. Watch carefully, or you will have a firsthand view of the Maillard reaction (burnt and crispy).

Note: Most of my recipes are very loose, as I frequently experiment and encourage others to do so. Failures are frequent but can be fun. Keep a fire extinguisher handy.

DEATH IN THE LAKE DISTRICT

CHAPTER ONE

My phone rang, and I looked at the screen. I rarely answered calls anymore unless I knew the caller, and I felt like it. Today's call satisfied neither requirement. Not only was it a number I didn't recognize, it was an unusual format and one I had not seen in a while. I immediately registered the +44 prefix in front of 4 digits, a space, then six digits as a call from the UK. It had been a few years and a career ago since any business associates called me from there. I held the phone for a minute to see if there was a voicemail notification, but there was not. Filing it under mildly interesting, I pocketed the phone, and went back to hacking weeds out of the community garden. I had about twenty more minutes of manual labor before the chore was finished.

Back home after a shower, I fixed dinner and sat on the porch. I thought about calling Donna, but I was not sure she was back and recovered from her book tour yet. She had been on a driving tour around the southeast, mostly towns and small cities. Then she ended the tour with large shows in Atlanta and Dallas. It sounded like more fun than it was. A new town and a new hotel every night, with a reading and book signing every day. It would be tedious, but it was necessary to keep her readers satiated. She had not asked me to go, and I was grateful for her not asking. I missed her, but she probably knew the trip was not going to be fun. We still spent time together, but neither of us had figured out where this relationship was going. Or maybe she had, but not told me yet. I was usually the last to know about any relationship status.

Otherwise life had gotten quiet again after the kerfuffle with the rogue sheriff and the vicious tow truck driver. The drug-running sheriff was doing twenty years in prison, along with two of his deputies, and Doyle the car tower and murderer was dead. The county was now a better place regarding both outcomes.

I decided a walk was in my future, so I asked Kat for permission to leave. She did not respond at first, then got up and trilled on the way to the refrigerator. That was my cue to bribe her acquiescence with roast chicken. That done, I was on my way.

Passing the once beautiful, now rotting cottages along the outer loop of the campus always gave me a feeling of despair. Part of the Roosevelt Warm Springs, or RWS campus, the cottages had been built anywhere from 70 to 90 years ago for people living and working on campus. But once the owners left, the cottages were held empty and abandoned by the state, since they remained state property. A lot of history and aesthetic architecture was slowly turning to dust.

As I made my way along the outer loop road, I came to

one cottage that was in private ownership and still inhabited. My friend Millard, more than eighty years old, made it his kingdom. The side-by-side utility vehicle, street legal at least in Warm Springs, was out front, so he was home. I had given it to him so he could get around easier on and off campus with his bad hip. I saw him step onto his porch with a pitcher of something resembling lemonade and knew I was right on time.

"James, come up and have a shot of vitamin C," he said.

"Thanks Millard, I believe I will."

We sat in the rocking chairs and enjoyed the sweet-sour lemonade on ice. Just one sprig of mint to give it the slightest hint of exotic.

"You've been awfully quiet these days," Millard said. "No murder, mayhem, or ruckus at all that you've been associated with. Makes me think you are planning something."

"Millard, all I'm planning is how to make more money from a bookstore and what to plant next in the campus community garden."

"That is terribly boring. Not even a wedding on the horizon?" I gave him my best withering look. It didn't work. "Poor girl didn't throw you over for some wealthy baseball player, did she? Or find a match out on her tour?"

"Not that I am aware of. We are still seeing each other. But like everything else lately, it's been slow."

"The shiny days have worn off and you don't know what to do with the patina, now do you?"

"Never heard it put quite like that, but maybe so."

"You will need to jumpstart those lusty urges back to

the early days. Before she got to see your used toothbrush on the vanity."

"Thanks for your input, but that is not the problem."

"Then what is? You can tell old uncle Millard. Sometimes I might even give you good advice."

"I'm not really sure. She's a great person and wonderful company. The problem is me."

"Oh, got it. You don't think you are worthy, or you looking to shop in another supermarket?"

"Neither. I think I'm bored, floating in a doldrum of life at the moment. Not even Donna has pulled me out, and it's certainly not her duty to do so anyway."

"Have you told her?"

"No, but I think she knows something is wrong. Although it is not like anything is wrong, except for my attitude."

"You best get to talking to her. As a woman, she might think you've lost interest in her, so she will protect her emotions. You will be on the outs because you have a pouty attitude. Dumb way to lose her."

"I have to admit you are right. She should be home and rested up from the tour. As soon as I finish the lemonade, I'm going to start walking and call her."

"Don't wait. There is always more lemonade where this came from. But there aren't that many nice people out there that like you."

"Excellent point. Thanks Millard, I'll be going now."

"Good luck and don't screw it up. Can't have you moping all over my porch now that I have a social life."

I believe he was giving me the bum's rush because he

had company coming over or had a date in town. When I got to the end of his driveway, I called Donna.

"Hi there. Do you have time to talk?"

"Hi James. On the phone or somewhere else?"

"Somewhere else. Anywhere you would like."

"How about your front porch? I need something quiet after the last three weeks."

"Sounds great."

"I'll be there in thirty minutes."

I was already feeling better. Now I just had to decide how to tell Donna I was floating in a dead zone that had nothing to do with her.

I had put out two cold drinks on the porch when Donna drove up. She gave me a quick peck, more reminiscent of a friend than anything more. Maybe I had waited too long.

"Thanks for coming over."

"Sure James. It sounded like you needed to talk."

"I do. I stopped by to see Millard while out walking. He asked me what was wrong. I wasn't sure or really even thinking about. But I realized he was right, that I might be acting off."

"You are definitely off. I think it started about two months ago. Almost to the point I was going to say something, but I decided to wait until after I got back."

"You noticed too?"

"Of course I did. What is wrong?"

"I feel like I'm adrift in the Sargasso Sea. Not much happening and I'm stuck in a boring place in my life. Not you or my friends, that is all good. But my daily life is wonderful yet not very exciting."

"I suspect you are a bit of an adventure junky. But you now live in a tiny town with little happening, and own one of the least adventurous businesses known to humankind."

"What do I do to break out of the slump?"

"You need more excitement. Even more than what I can provide as your girlfriend."

"Are you my girlfriend?"

"I believe so. All the facts point toward it being true. Do you want to be my boyfriend?"

"I think so."

She made a bad buzzer noise. "Brrruurrzzz. Wrong answer. You have one more chance."

"Yes, I want to. But I don't know how to make it work."

"You don't make it work. We make it work, up to the point that one or both of us would rather floss with barbed wire than keep going."

"In that case, as my official girlfriend, I now entrust you with exciting me."

"You know how lame that sounds, right?"

"I do, but it was so bad I really needed to say it."

"Let's get you to an adventure, preferably one where you don't have to talk. It does not have to be a murder, does it? I'm fresh out of those, thankfully."

"Aww, I was hoping for murder. But mayhem would do nicely."

"What have you done for excitement in the past? There must have been something you enjoyed before chasing murderers."

"In my younger days, I went hunting and fishing. Then I realized how silly and sad that was. Not for me, but for the dead animals that resulted. Other things have come and gone. Maybe the only thing left in my external life is traveling. Have you ever been to Alaska?"

"I have not, but always wanted to go. Are you asking me?"

"I believe so. Or are there other places you would like to go?"

"I have a long list. I traveled some while married and liked it. I would like to go see the western US, Alaska, several Caribbean islands, and about anywhere in Europe."

"Not Hawaii?"

"Been there on a honeymoon. Liked it, but don't need to go back until I've seen everything else on the list."

"I feel the same way. Nice, but there are lots of other places to go."

"Let me think about it for a while. I'll come up with a top five list, and you do the same. If we have matches, we can set up a trip."

"I like that. It sounds so mature that two people can make rational decisions."

"Keep that mature talk to yourself. I'm still thirty-nine."

"Do you have any minimum requirements?"

"Some place that does not require prior immunizations, and wherever we go I need a fully functional bathroom with shower."

"I can go along with that. Somewhere with adequate facilities and no epidemics. I'll add jungle to the do not go list. Heat, humidity, bugs and snakes don't sound fun."

"Me either. The jungle would not be good for my hair. Now, will a trip get you back to normal?"

"Can't hurt, as it should reset my dour meter."

"Yes, let's have all that dour go away. But to reset my dour meter, what kind of dinner can you feed me?"

"I'll find something to make you happy. If I didn't know better, I'd think you wanted to meet here so you could persuade me to fix you dinner."

"You do know better, and that's exactly why we met here. I have not had a decent home-cooked meal in weeks."

"Well then, I will make something worthy of your feminine wiles."

"Thank you, James. Now get to it, and how can I help?"

www.ingramcontent.com/pod-product-compliance
Lightning Source LLC
Chambersburg PA
CBHW031026310726
48969CB00007B/1882